POISONED HARMONY
THE COMPLETE CASES OF THE
SCIENTIFIC CLUB, VOLUME 2

POISONED HARMONY

THE COMPLETE CASES OF THE SCIENTIFIC CLUB, VOLUME 2

RAY CUMMINGS

ILLUSTRATED BY

F.M. FOLLETT
FRANK R. PAUL

COVER BY

LEJAREN HILLER

POPULAR PUBLICATIONS · 2023

TABLE OF CONTENTS

TELLING WHAT HE KNEW

"MR. OBER WILL tell you all he knows of the affair, gentlemen," said the Chemist. "His wife has vanished—"

The Banker interrupted. "When did she vanish? Isn't this a matter for the police?"

"Quite so," agreed the Chemist. "The police are working on it, of course. Mr. Ober reported to them at once—a week, nearly ten days ago now—the morning he awakened to find his wife gone."

The Alienist said: "Tell them the details, Rogers."

And the Banker put in: "You brought us the case, Rogers? You knew the woman personally?"

"An acquaintance merely," said the Chemist. "These are the details, gentlemen." He turned to the club's visitor. "You will pardon me if I speak frankly, Mr. Ober. It is necessary, if we are to help you."

The visitor nodded. "Yes, I don't mind."

He was a man of about forty—small, dark, and wiry; a thin, smooth shaven face with a muddy, sallow skin; slightly bald, with brown patches like overgrown freckles on his forehead and scalp. He had a furtive, nervous manner, and peering little black eyes. As he spoke he smiled slightly, and his thin fingers twisted themselves in his lap. He was an Austrian, but long residence in America had worn his accent smooth.

The Chemist nodded. "Thanks." His gaze swung back to

the group of men in the clubroom. "The case is this, gentlemen, very briefly. Professor Wallace and I, as you know, live
in Westchester—in Bedfordville. So also do Mr. and Mrs.
Ober. She was an American—he is an Austrian.

"I give you now the circumstances as the police claim
them to be, without regard to Mr. Ober's feelings. He
married his wife about six years ago. She was a widow
some fifty-five years of age; that is to say, fifteen years
his senior. Not very—excuse me, Mr. Ober—I mean to
say, she was physically rather unattractive. She had some
money when they were married which, the police allege,
he spent rather rapidly. After which, it is also alleged, they
quarreled frequently. Neighbors' gossip, you understand,
which, in spite of Mr. Ober's denial, the police claim to
have unearthed."

The Astronomer spoke up. "You mean, Rogers, that Mr.
Ober is suspected of this crime?"

"We do not know that there has been a crime," the
Chemist said quickly. "Ten days ago Mr. Ober went to
bed as usual. He occupied a room adjoining that of his
wife. He slept soundly. In the morning he awakened to find
her gone. She left no message or reason and she has not
been heard from since. That's all there is to it. There were
no unusual circumstances between them the night before.
No quarrel, was there, Mr. Ober?"

"No—no. Nothing," the visitor answered. His glance
darted about the room. "Nothing. She was not sick—not
anything. And in that morning she was vanished."

"In the clothes she had been wearing the evening before,"
the Chemist added. "Just those garments were gone—
nothing else of her personal belongings. The house had not

*The Very Young Man sat on the arm of
the chair, glaring menacingly.*

been broken into. It seemed exactly as it had been the night before, except that the front door was unlocked. Quite as though Mrs. Ober had got up, dressed, and walked out. That's all. And now the police seem to suspect Mr. Ober. He is worried over his wife, naturally, and this attitude of the police is additionally distressing."

"If there has been no crime, what is he suspected of?" the Banker demanded.

Ober started to speak, but the Chemist answered for him. "Of complicity in her disappearance. There may have been a crime, the police say. An abduction, for instance." The Chemist shrugged his shoulders. "There is no one else handy for the police to suspect, and since they can't seem to find her, they are trying to take it out on him."

The Alienist said: "We had thought of somnambulism—"

"That might be the answer," the Banker exclaimed, but the Chemist shook his head.

"Or perhaps she was a victim of aphasia," suggested the Lawyer.

"We don't think it very probable," said the Chemist. "A level-headed, well-balanced woman. They mean, Mr. Ober, your wife never walked in her sleep, or had any mental trouble, loss of memory or anything like that?"

"No," declared Ober emphatically. "She was of good health. I was the one who is sick sometimes."

The Chemist went on: "I have told Mr. Ober that we of the Scientific Club here are sometimes able to work out problems of this sort. Not only does he wish to find his wife and get her back safely, but if some crime has occurred—an abduction he and I think it was—he wishes to run it to earth. The police are harassing him with their unjust suspicions—he wants to extricate himself from that also. And I have told him that possibly we can help him—here, tonight."

"How?" the Banker demanded. "You mean, without knowing any more of the affair than this, that we can do something about it—here, tonight—and find out what happened to this woman?"

"I think so, yes. Science advances. It must. The scientific resources of yesterday are child's play compared to the wonders of today and the seeming miracles of tomorrow. I feel that we may be able—this evening in the next hour or two—to apply our modern science in a way to throw light upon this problem. That is why Mr. Ober is here, and with the help of you gentleman—"

"You have a plan, Rogers?" the Doctor suggested. His glance at the Chemist seemed to imply far more than the words.

"Yes, Frank, I have. That is, I should say, Professor Wallace has." The Chemist's gesture went to the gray-haired, gray-bearded man beside him. "Allen, will you tell them?"

"I think you're doing very well," the older man said with a slow, quiet smile.

"Thanks, I'll proceed then. Let us assume, gentlemen, that Mrs. Ober has been abducted. In that event it is logical to assume also that in her mind at this present moment is the full knowledge of what has happened to her. None of us in this room has that knowledge, but she has it, and if we can get it from her—well, the problem, so far as we are concerned, is solved."

The scientists glanced at each other, but no one spoke. Ober sat nervously twisting his fingers, hitching his slight body in his chair, but his gleaming eyes clung to the Chemist's face.

"Telepathy, gentlemen," the Chemist said suddenly. "The power one mind has to communicate its thoughts to another. Professor Wallace, of everyone in America, I think, is an authority on telepathy."

The Chemist's gesture was deprecating. "I shall explain very badly, in comparison with him, but at least I shall have the merit of brevity. I went over all this with you yesterday, Mr. Ober, but still I want you to listen closely."

The Austrian's prominent Adam's apple bobbed as he gulped. "Yes—yes. I listen very hard. She was abducted. If you could prove—"

"We will try. Telepathy, as we know it today, is not, as popularly supposed, the thought-transference of definite ideas. It is generally something much more vague—

the transference merely of *impressions*. It is a much more common thing than the layman realizes.

"How often we feel depressed, for no apparent reason. We have vague premonitions of something impending, or of something having gone wrong with those dear to us far away! All that is usually telepathy, gentlemen!

"These moods, these premonitions, seem to us illogical, inspired within ourselves. They are not that. In nearly every case they originate elsewhere—in the subconscious mind of someone dear to us who has good reason to be depressed, or feel something impending. There are thought vibrations received by us from the mind of someone with whom we have been closely associated.

"I am speaking now of involuntary telepathy between those who have never practiced it—who do not even realize they have the power. You see my point? The knowledge of what has happened to Mrs. Ober is in her mind at this present moment. We want that knowledge and we can get it only one way, by having it transferred to the mind of Mr. Ober, and thence to us."

The Chemist's gesture and his warning glance silenced several questions. "Just a moment longer, please. If Mr. Ober were to think very hard, *Where are you?* we might expect that the answering thought would come to him, for instance, *Cranford, New Jersey.* Not so. It is far more elusive than that.

"She is thinking of her husband constantly, of course. And if his mind is relaxed—as receptive as possible—*impressions* of what she is thinking, of what has happened to her, of her present situation, will seep into his subconscious mind. They are already doing so, in fact.

"He is convinced that she has been abducted. There is no evidence of it—no known motive for anyone to abduct her. Yet he is convinced. Why? Because his subconscious mind has already received it from hers.

"With the proper care, gentlemen, we can get these impressions from his subconscious mind, sort them out, interpret them, let me say. Piece them together by logical reasoning until we have the complete story of what has happened to her. Allen, may I have your papers?"

The Professor produced a sheaf of four or five long, narrow pages. The Chemist rustled them, adjusting his horn-rimmed spectacles.

"I have here a list of words prepared by Professor Wallace. They are abstract, apparently unrelated words, but very carefully selected, I assure you. Some two hundred of them." He raised the pages to the light. "They run like this: *House. Tree. Door. Train. Village. Dress. Boat.* Apparently unrelated, as you observe, but they are not so. In their entirety they cover every phase of what we conceive may be Mrs. Ober's present situation.

"These words will be read slowly one by one to Mr. Ober. For instance, we read: *House.* His mind thinking of that will send the *impression* of a house to the subconscious mind of Mrs. Ober. To her, that impression may stimulate the thought of her home in Bedfordville. Or the mansion or the shack in which she may now be confined. We do not know.

"But whatever thought is awakened, an *impression* of that thought, let me repeat, will almost instantly revert to the subconscious mind of Mr. Ober. Thought processes are very rapid; a second or two, no more, for the complete process."

"Interesting," murmured the Banker. "But in practice—how are we going to operate it?"

"Like this. Listen closely, Mr. Ober. You will recline in your chair. Professor Wallace will read you his list of words. After each word, without conscious thought—understand that, you are not to think of anything voluntarily—after each word you are to speak *at once* the first word that comes to your mind. Whatever it may be, speak it out.

"For instance, if when Professor Wallace says *House* you happen to think of *Shack* or *Hospital,* for instance, whatever it is, say it aloud at once. Don't stop to think. If you do, we will have only your own thought—not your wife's. Do you understand me?"

Ober was convinced that he did, but very carefully the Chemist repeated his instructions. The Austrian was obviously eager to start. "She is abducted," he said. "I know it. I feel it, and if we can make it into proof—"

"Yes," agreed the Chemist, "that is our object."

The Alienist rose abruptly from his chair and crossed over to the Chemist. "Very good, Rogers," he whispered. "You're putting it very well, indeed."

The Very Young Man, with flushed cheeks, was plainly excited. He met the Chemist's glance and jumped up eagerly.

"The screen, Jack," said the Chemist. And to the room: "Will you gentlemen move aside? I want space, to put that screen about Mr. Ober's chair. We must have him secluded—his mind must be perfectly at rest."

The Very Young Man brought the screen, standing it

around Ober's big leather chair. It secluded three sides, while in front Professor Wallace sat facing it with his papers in hand. Within the shelter of the screen, Ober reclined at ease. His elbows were on the broad chair arms, his hands to his face.

"Is it right what I am doing?" he asked. "I try hard, Mr. Rogers—Professor Wallace—to make of your experiment a success."

"Quite right," smiled the Chemist. "Now—the lights, Jack. Get them lower—I want you thoroughly relaxed, Mr. Ober. As though you were half dozing, listening to the words Professor Wallace gives you, and answering at once the first word—no matter what it is—that comes into your head."

The Very Young Man lowered the lights until all the room was in shadow. On a table beside Professor Wallace, a small shaded lamp illuminated his papers. Outside the screen, dispersed about the room, the scientists settled back to watch and listen, whispering among themselves until the Chemist silenced them.

During these moments Professor Wallace had been reiterating to Ober what he was to do. The Very Young Man simultaneously was moving quietly about the room. In a farther corner, some distance away from the screen, stood a soundproof telephone booth. The Very Young Man slipped into it, closed the door, and lifted the receiver.

"Irene?"

The telephone operator downstairs in the club lobby answered him. Then he said:

"Yes. Jack Bruce, Irene." His voice was low, but urgent and excited. "We're starting now. Mr. Rogers says get them on the wire out there right away.... Yes, hold them on the wire.... Yes, they expect that—they'll hold it all right.... I don't know. Maybe any time. Maybe not for an hour or two. But we'll be in a hurry—no time to bother with connections.... Yes, sure thing. I'll jump right in here whenever we get anything."

He hung up. Outside in the room, close up against the back of the screen, a small table with a shaded desk lamp on it had been placed. The Alienist sat there, with a pad of paper and a pencil before him.

The Very Young Man approached, whispering: "She'll hold them on the wire. Are we doing all right, Dr. Gregg?"

"Yes. Fine. You, Jack—you've got the watch?"

"Yes. Here it is." He placed a stopwatch on the table.

"Thanks. Mr. Grant is going to write them down. I'll keep the time." He made a place for the Big Business Man who took the pencil and pulled the pad before him.

The Very Young Man sat with them. "Good. I'll be needed for the telephone. When's he going to start?" Professor Wallace was still instructing Ober. The Chemist, hovering nearby, saw that the little group at the table were settled.

"All ready, Allen."

The Professor nodded. "Now, Mr. Ober—*House.*"

A brief silence. Ober stirred in his chair. "*Hospit*—I mean *shack.*"

"No, that won't do, Mr. Ober. You were trying to think of your answer. Which was it? Which word did you think of first?"

"*Shack,*" said Ober positively.

"Very well. Just relax now. You'll soon fall into it. And

if you tire, let me know. We can take an intermission at any time."

The reading proceeded. The room was dim and silent; the only sound was the droning of the Professor's voice as he softly and monotonously intoned the words and Ober's answers, sometimes halting, sometimes spontaneous.

The Chemist had joined those at the little table. The Big Business Man was writing down each word and the word Ober answered opposite it; with his stopwatch the Alienist was timing the intervals—the length of time it took for Ober's answer, which the Big Business Man also jotted down—one-half to nearly five seconds and occasionally when Ober stammered in doubt, more than ten seconds elapsed between the word and Ober's reaction.

The group at the table were shielded from Ober by the screen, and their low whispers could not reach him. Half an hour passed; evidently there were more words than the Chemist had stated, for the Professor's list seemed inexhaustible.

Abruptly the Chemist rose. The men at the table were whispering vehemently.

"Just a minute, Allen. Isn't Mr. Ober tiring?"

The Professor halted. "Yes, doubtless. Sit up, Mr. Ober. We will rest now for a few moments."

Ober sat up, rubbing his temples. "Is it working, Professor Wallace? I do my best. Do you know now, maybe, what happened to my wife?" His black eyes gleamed with eagerness; there seemed almost triumph in his tone.

In the gloom of the room, the Very Young Man was hastily threading his way between the chairs of silent spectators. He entered the telephone booth, closing its door soundlessly after him.

The Chemist approached the open side of the screen where the Professor was talking with Ober. The two scientists exchanged glances. The Chemist drew up a chair.

"You're doing very well, Mr. Ober," he said enthusiastically. "We're getting it. Not all of it yet—but a little. Piece by piece—and we're putting it together. Your wife was abducted—unquestionably."

"Ah!" exclaimed Ober. "That I was sure of!" Real triumph was in his tone. "What else, Mr. Rogers?"

"Abducted," repeated the Chemist. "A man—very big and burly—with a blond beard. And he took her on a train and boat, I suppose a ferryboat—we did not get that exactly. Took her to Cranford. You said *Cranford* in answer to the word *Town.* Obviously *Cranford,* New Jersey. A shack there. We assume she may be confined there now, in the outskirts somewhere."

Ober rubbed his lean hands. "Yes, that is it? Shall we go on, Professor Wallace?" He threw himself back in his chair in readiness.

"Shortly," the Chemist replied. "Dr. Gregg is analyzing your answers, he will be ready presently."

The Very Young Man had now emerged quietly from the telephone booth. He whispered with the Alienist, took a paper of notes, slipped back into the booth, and read them swiftly over the telephone. In another moment he was back in his place beside the table.

The Chemist stood up. "I think you may proceed, Allen."

The test began again. The period was longer than before,

and twice during it, the Very Young Man was at the telephone. Then, again, the Chemist called an intermission.

"We are coming along, Mr. Ober. Soon we shall have all the details. Are you tired?"

"No—no. Yes—perhaps a little tired."

Obviously the Austrian was tired. During the first session he had seemed very alert. But the monotony of the thing had lulled him. When he found that the experiment was to be a success, he seemed unconsciously to relax. He had hardly stirred in his chair throughout the second session; his answers came regularly, seemingly spontaneously for the most part, and without conscious effort.

The Chemist said: "Now, Mr. Ober, if you are ready. Just a little more and then we are through. We have almost the complete story now. This big blond giant abducted her. We have traced his movements—his motives almost. It is all in the answers you have already given, once we interpret them correctly. You need not worry any further, Mr. Ober."

Evidently Ober did not, for during the third session his answers came far more freely than before. Once the Alienist motioned vehemently to the Very Young Man, whispered to him, and the Very Young Man dashed excitedly to the telephone again. But Ober did not hear the slight noise he made, and the screen hid almost the entire room from the Austrian's view. The reading proceeded, until at last the Chemist stopped it.

"I think that is enough, Allen." The Chemist's voice was tense, but he was smiling. "Quite enough, Mr. Ober. And let me congratulate you. We have the story now—apparently complete."

The room stirred. The spectators were whispering, shifting their feet. The Banker said: "Rogers, if you—"

"Not now, George," warned the Chemist sharply. "You may turn on the lights, Jack. But I must ask all you gentlemen to remain quiet. We must wait—"

The Very Young Man switched on the lights. The men sat blinking. At the little table the Alienist was poring over his voluminous notes—comparing words, constructing sentences, impressions, ideas.

Over two hours had passed since the experiment was first begun. Another long interval went by, while the Professor and the Chemist engaged Ober in low-toned conversation. Ober was triumphant. This blond giant with the beard had abducted his wife, taken her to Cranford, New Jersey, where she was, or had been, confined in a shack.

"But I feel that now maybe he has taken her somewhere else, very far away," Ober insisted. "Maybe soon we will hear she is dead. Maybe we could get proof of that some time, Mr. Rogers."

The Chemist nodded. "That would be unfortunate. But you, Mr. Ober, you will be released from suspicion, at least."

"Yes—yes."

The Very Young Man had left the door of the telephone booth slightly ajar. The telephone bell rang now—rang through the room insistently, startlingly loud. The Chemist jumped to his feet and ran to answer the summons. He was in the booth, with the door closed tightly upon him, for no more than a moment, but when he returned to the room his face was white and set. He stopped at the table and spoke in a swift, triumphant undertone to the Alienist. Together they went to the opening of the screen.

The Chemist said: "An outside call, Mr. Ober. Nothing important."

He quietly removed the screen. Ober sat around to face the room, glowing at the idea that he was the center of all eyes, and the Chemist stood close beside him.

The spectators were tense. The Banker blurted out: "Rogers, for Heaven's sake—" But the Chemist's raised hand and quiet voice checked him.

"I shall explain now, for those of you who do not already understand. Gentlemen, we have now the story of the disappearance of Mrs. Ober." He paused slightly. "Mr. Ober's answered words fall into several classifications— none of them clearly defined—with exceptions to each classification, but in general, easily recognizable. There were, first, the words which proved to have no bearing upon the case whatever.

"To this largest class, Mr. Ober gave answer in from one-half to one second, seldom more. The words he gave seemed to have no bearing upon each other. There was no story to tell—no inferences of any story to be drawn from them. There were no *unusual* answers in this class. Each one was readily and obviously inspired merely by the word from Professor Wallace.

"This class Dr. Gregg discarded. Of the remaining minority, there were a number which seemed to link themselves together into the story of an abduction, the blond, bearded giant, train, boat, Cranford, the shack, and all the rest of it. Almost without exception these words took *five seconds* or more.

"Delayed answers are obviously the result of conscious thought. Also they nearly all came in the first session when

Mr. Ober was alert and vigilant. More than that, each of them constituted an unusual answer to the keyword—and an illogical answer, psychologically incorrect, if I may use such a term."

The smug triumph was fading from Ober's face. He looked bewildered, vaguely alarmed. The Chemist raised his voice slightly as he continued:

"This class of words, gentlemen, this whole story of the abduction—obviously represented Ober's effort to trick us. That was why he welcomed this test. He figured we were deluding ourselves with our science, and our evidence to the police would throw them off the scent and release himself from suspicion. Later, he would trump up some evidence that his wife was dead, and marry a certain young Austrian widow—with money. We can only infer his motives. They are really not interesting or important. We deal with facts—"

The Austrian was on his feet, but the Chemist waved him back.

"Sit down! You'll—"

"It is a lie! You think you can—"

"Trap you?" asked the Chemist more quietly. "Surprise you into a confession? Not at all. In fact, very stupid. We want no confession from you—it isn't necessary."

Evidently Ober thought that in this crisis he had best remain silent. He sat quiet, sullen, but his glance roved involuntarily toward the door, as though he longed to escape.

The Chemist went on, speaking somewhat faster: "This has not been a test of telepathy, gentlemen, and Professor Wallace has had no more to do with it than the reading of the words. The list was prepared by Dr. Gregg, a purely psychological test which he has studied very closely and has used scores of times in his daily routine. He was in my office yesterday, when I interviewed Ober, sizing Ober up, let me say.

"Ober is an unusual type, quick, nervous manner, and yet a stupid, unimaginative mind. He is smugly complacent, not the sort you could trap into a confession. So Dr. Gregg planned this test—this different sort of trap—in which we let Ober think he could trick us to his own advantage— Sit down, Mr. Ober! You had better keep silent and hear me out!

"Dr. Gregg, then, discarded all the words which told the story of an abduction. It was all false from every angle. I suggested to Ober yesterday that his wife might have been abducted. Tonight I casually named Cranford. Quite a coincidence that she should then be shown to have been abducted and that Cranford should be the exact place! We know that this was because Ober is too unimaginative to invent other things in the few seconds he had between words.

"I even suggested *Shack* to him, you'll remember. He seized it, and it has figured very prominently ever since. And this blond, bearded giant, Ober's exact physical opposite! Such a blatant effort to divert suspicion from himself is characteristic of his mentality and is in itself indicative of guilt.

"So, with the abduction discarded, we had left a third and last class of words—the answers by which Ober unwittingly gave us the real story!…Jack, suppose you sit by Mr. Ober? I want him to stay where he is—not leave his chair!"

The Very Young Man sat on the arm of Ober's chair, glaring at him menacingly.

"Thanks," smiled the Chemist. "The problem, gentlemen, was not at all as I stated it to you for Ober's benefit. Dr. Gregg and I offered to help the police. We suspected that Ober was at the bottom of his wife's disappearance. The evidence against him would never convict, it hardly warranted an arrest. He was not the sort the police could overawe—just clever enough to appear wholly dumb.

"Why was he so strongly suspected? Two small bits of evidence which he does not yet know the police obtained. A neighbor heard his automobile start out in the middle of the night—the night his wife disappeared. It was gone nearly an hour, then it came back.... Oh, yes; we knew that, Mr. Ober. Your wife's abductor would hardly bring the car back. And you never mentioned having been out yourself—in fact, you stated quite the contrary. No, never mind now!

"The other point, gentlemen, is that since the disappearance Ober has constantly been shadowed by the police. He visited, a few days ago, a woman here in New York, a young, rather beautiful Austrian widow—with money. The police assume she is to be Mrs. Ober's successor. That's enough, Jack! I'm sure he'll sit quiet.

"The third class of words gave us the real story. It came during Ober's relaxed, unguarded moments. It was all seething in his mind—the story of what he really did that night. It was inevitable that with such a test, prepared by the trained mind of Dr. Gregg, some of the real story should slip out. A detached word here and there, none of which to Ober seemed significant or dangerous.

"But they were nearly all easily recognizable. Nearly all were answers of one second or less. Thus, spontaneous. They were unusual words also—unusual, I mean, in relation to their keywords—answers which never could have sprung from a normal, innocent mind free of secret, guilty knowledge.

"More than that, as we began to get fragments, hints here and there of the real story, we could see keywords coming which occasionally hit the guilty facts closely and obviously. Several of these Ober recognized and avoided. He stirred in his chair, his answer was greatly delayed; and when the answer finally came it was invariably wholly irrelevant.

"For instance, at the keyword *Murder*, Ober evidently did not like his thoughts. He hesitated some twelve seconds, and then he said, '*Bird.*' Totally abnormal. In the mind of an innocent man, the word 'murder' might conceivably inspire a variety of chance thoughts, but 'bird' would hardly be one of them.

"So this sort of answer gave us also a variety of indirect information. Inferences are not difficult to a mind as trained and skilled as that of Dr. Gregg. He got no complete story. That is impossible. But it gave him enough hints—and we have acted upon them.

"For nearly three hours now, that telephone over there has been connected with the police station in Bedfordville. A busy evening this, in Bedfordville. A score or more private automobiles and drivers have been volunteered by the residents up there. They have been at the police station all evening, waiting for hints, clues, from us.

"These were searching parties, gentlemen! We very soon

had indications in this test that Ober murdered his wife—
Easy, Jack, don't hurt him! We assumed that he had taken
her body off in his car to hide it—make away with it. The
car was gone less than an hour—he could not have traveled very far.

"So tonight we arranged searching parties—a score of
them—for we wanted to find the body. At every hint we
could draw from Ober, Bedfordville has been notified, and
a car or two has started off to run down the clue.

"There was a railroad bridge. A pile of stones. An old
house. A tree, willow, at a brookside. And by the stones, a
broad patch of sand. Easy for digging! To dig through turf
and tree-roots is difficult. All these things and a variety
of others, Dr. Gregg pieced together by inference from
abnormalities of words and time-intervals. The searching parties have all the evening been following every
possible clue. Some inferences Dr. Gregg doubtless made
wrongly. Others were right. And when the 'phone rang a
few moments ago, I learned—"

A knock on the door checked the Chemist—a club
attendant with whom he whispered. The door closed as
the attendant departed.

The Chemist said briskly: "No more, gentleman. Visitors
downstairs—they are coming up. In a word, Bedfordville
has found the body of Mrs. Ober, murdered in her night-
gown, wrapped in a blood-soaked blanket, buried with
the knife with which she was stabbed, and with a pile of
clothes—the clothes she had worn the evening before!"

Ober was out of his chair, struggling with the muscular
Very Young Man.

"It is a lie! You never can prove anything against me! You—"

"Oh, yes, we can," retorted the Chemist. "There seems plenty of ordinary police evidence about the body and weapon. And you forget, Dr. Gregg drew it all from your own mid. It all originated there—your own guilty knowledge—"

The door opened; police from the nearby New York station were in the room. The Chemist advance to meet them.

"There's your man," he said.

WHEN ROSA CONFESSED

"YOU SAY THIS Rosa Vitelli has confessed to the murder," exclaimed the Banker. "There's no mystery when you have a—"

The Doctor nodded. "Quite so. But, gentlemen, though she admits having killed the girl Angelina, she will not tell how she did it. There is considerable mystery about that."

The Doctor gazed around the small private clubroom, with its group of interested members; and then indicated the two visitors beside him. He added: "Mr. Green and Sergeant Marberry here are puzzled. More than that—"

"Suppose you give us an outline of the case," the Chemist interrupted. "If you think we can be of any help—"

"I will. As I told you, Sergeant Marberry, a good friend of mine, has been assigned to this Vitelli affair. Because of his knowledge of Italian he is very frequently given such cases. And Mr. Green, one of the assistant district attorneys, has the case in his office for prosecution."

The Banker raised his hand impatiently. "The murder, Frank—"

"Quite so," smiled the Doctor. "Briefly, the circumstances are these: Some three weeks ago—on the early morning of January 10th, to be exact—a young Italian girl was found dead. She lived in the Italian section south of Greenwich Village. Name, Angelina Torno. Age, twenty-three. Unmarried. An extremely pretty girl—a factory worker.

"With another girl roommate, she occupied a small flat on the third floor of a tenement building. This other girl does not enter the case—she had been on Staten Island with a sick mother for several weeks, leaving Angelina alone in the flat.

"On the early morning of January 10th, one of the fourth floor tenants came downstairs, and in the dim, badly ventilated third floor hallway, smelled gas. There is no electric light in this building; all gas. Angelina did not answer thumps upon her door. It was later broken in. Her flat was found flooded with gas, and the girl in bed—dead."

"Suicide!" murmured the Banker. "You said murder—"

The Doctor smiled grimly. "Wait, George. It was murder, not suicide. The night of January 9th and 10th was extremely cold—you all remember that three-day cold spell we had. Angelina slept that night with all her windows closed—even the transom over her door to the public hall was closed. All the doors and windows closed and locked on the inside.

"The outside temperature was down to zero that night. It was perfectly natural for an Italian girl to shut herself up without fresh air and go to bed.

"But it was murder, not suicide, for though the little flat was full of gas and the girl dead of asphyxiation, every gas cock in the flat was turned off securely. That was not suicide, gentlemen. You don't kill yourself by turning on the gas and then get up and turn it off."

The Astronomer murmured: "But how—"

"Exactly so." The Doctor glanced at his watch. "I must

hasten—Jack, are you and Professor Walton ready with everything?"

The Very Young Man nodded eagerly. "Yes, sir. Everything's ready."

"Good. Gentlemen, this Rosa Vitelli is in custody. Mr. Green has ordered her brought here tonight—they will have her here any moment. In a word, the Vitellis occupied the third floor flat across the hall from Angelina. A young, rather well educated Italian-American couple. Rosa, eighteen; and Georgio, twenty-six. Married just over a year. No children.

"Sergeant Marberry here was assigned to the case. Marberry established at once that young Vitelli had been paying undue attention to the Torno girl—so much so that he and his wife had had violent quarrels over it.

"After the murder, when the Vitellis were about to be arrested, Rosa gave way under Mr. Green's questioning and confessed. Jealousy was her motive. She was afraid she would lose her husband to the other girl. And doubtless she had good reason to suppose so.

"All that is clear enough. The queer part is that Rosa absolutely refuses to tell how she committed the murder. Nothing can break down that refusal. If, by some unknown method she got into Angelina's flat, turned on the gas, and then turned it off and got out again, how she could leave the doors and windows locked on the inside, with a key on the inside lock of the only hall door—all this she refuses to explain."

"Why won't she explain?" the Alienist demanded.

"There you have it! Why won't she? That also, we do do not know. But she will not. Her husband possibly could tell how she did it, but he maintains only a stubborn, sullen silence and says he does not know."

Sergeant Marberry, a slender, dark-haired man nearing forty, said abruptly: "You have not told them, Dr. Adams, that we think we know how the crime was committed. This Rosa Vitelli—"

The Doctor interrupted. "Sergeant Marberry has unearthed a few other facts which might be used against the Vitelli girl to break her down. But it is only theory— not proof—and the difficulty is that if he and Mr. Green used them and Rosa did not break down, nothing could ever be accomplished."

"I don't understand," the Banker exclaimed. "This girl has confessed to a murder. Why not go ahead and sentence her? Why bother with *how* she did it?"

"You'll see in a moment, George. It is a problem Mr. Green has several times had to face, particularly in dealing with Italians. Let me go on. Three significant facts were brought to light. One: a fourth floor tenant over the Vitelli flat, noticed that night a peculiar smell coming up. Something burning—a stench—"

"Burning a body!" the Banker ejaculated.

"George, don't be absurd. Angelina's body was found peacefully in bed—asphyxiated. The second fact, gentlemen: Whenever a peculiar, novel and yet simple crime is committed, other criminals imitate it.

"You remember the 'poison needle' craze that swept over the country some years ago? And when bichloride of mercury once got publicity as a comfortable means of suicide, it was used widely."

"You mean that somebody has already imitated this crime?" the Banker demanded.

"I do not. I mean that Sergeant Marberry felt at once

*On the floor lay the struggling forms of the
husband and the Very Young Man.*

that this crime might be in imitation of a previous one.
Where would Rosa Vitelli get the ingenuity to plan it? To
originate it? Sergeant Marberry guessed that she did not.
Purely a guess, but on the chance, he searched all the New
York newspapers of the previous few days.

"He found what he was looking for. On January 7th,
in the Bronx, an attempted murder almost asphyxiated a
whole family. Understand me, I don't mean to imply that
this had any connection with the Vitellis—except to give
Rosa the inspiration as to how she might murder Angelina.
This Bronx affair concerned obscure people—and since no
one was injured it occupied very little news space.

"None of you gentlemen noticed it, perhaps. But
Sergeant Marberry did, and he saw in it an explanation of
this murder of Angelina Torno."

Several of the club members interrupted with questions,
but the Doctor ignored them.

2

"IF ROSA VITELLI read that little news item—and possibly she did since it was also run in the Italian paper which the Vitellis are in the habit of buying—then we can assume that she might easily have been prompted to imitate it. The circumstances were the same, and—"

"What circumstances?" demanded the Chemist. "You don't mean the motives?"

"No, I mean the method by which the murder was committed." The Doctor took a newspaper clipping from his pocket. "Here it is, read it. And then I'll tell you a surprising suspicion which Mr. Green and Sergeant Marberry feel is close to the real truth."

A knock sounded on the clubroom door. The Doctor hastily disposed of his clipping. "No more now, gentlemen. You'll have to wait. Just sit quietly and watch. They're here, Sergeant Marberry."

The door had opened. Two policemen and a blond, stocky young man in civilian clothes entered with the girl Rosa Vitelli. And with them another young man, tall and dark, Georgio Vitelli, husband of Rosa.

The blond young man from the assistant district attorney's office greeted his superior, and with a low command seated Rosa in a chair facing the Doctor. Her husband sat near her; the two policemen retired unobtrusively to the other side of the room and sat down, staring around curiously.

Very briefly the Doctor introduced the newcomers; and then standing over Rosa, he abruptly demanded:

"We want to know how you killed Angelina. Will you tell us now?"

"No," she said sullenly, with her gaze on the floor. She was a small, dark-haired girl, typically Italian-American. Pretty in a pale, bedraggled fashion. She sat hunched in her chair, staring stolidly at the floor by the Doctor's feet.

"You won't?" he reiterated sharply.

No answer.

"Rosa, look up here."

Her gaze came reluctantly up to his face.

"Rosa, why won't you?"

Still no answer. The Doctor shifted his question; his tone became less harsh.

"*Why* did you kill Angelina? You'll tell these gentlemen *that*, won't you?"

"Yes," she said. Her dark eyes flashed; color flooded into her pale cheeks. She burst out passionately: "Angelina steal my Georgio. You know that! Everybody knows it. And so I kill her!"

The girl's eyes turned toward her handsome young husband and they softened with tenderness. "She—that Angelina—make love to my Georgio. And so I kill her."

"Gad," murmured the Astronomer to the man beside him. "She may have had good reason, from her viewpoint, to kill that other girl. The sympathetic type—it's lucky she confessed, you'd never get a jury to convict a girl like that.

And where are you going to get a judge to sentence her very heavily?"

The assistant district attorney heard the comments and flashed a warning glance. The Doctor was persisting:

"Yes, Rosa, we understand that. But you know it's wrong to kill, don't you?"

Her gaze again had fallen.

"Don't you?"

She burst out: "No! That Angelina do wrong—she steal my husband. I tol' her to let him alone."

"How did you kill her, Rosa? You planned it ahead of time, didn't you? I say you planned it very carefully, didn't you?"

Silence.

"You won't tell?"

"No."

"Why not? Why are you afraid to let us know how you did it?"

Still no answer. And abruptly the girl looked up with a glance almost of appeal.

"Why won't you tell, Rosa?"

The Astronomer leaned toward the assistant district attorney. "She's been advised against it. Knows you're trying to establish premeditation."

"Yes—of course. But that doesn't apply to the first moment of her confession. She was almost hysterical—and she isn't clever enough to think of a thing like that. Sh!"

"We're going to make you tell," the Doctor was saying gruffly. "That's why we brought you here."

It startled the girl. She gripped the sides of her chair with her small white hands.

Georgio exclaimed: "You let my Rosa alone! I will get

her lawyer." He started to his feet toward a telephone across the room, but the Doctor waved him back.

"Sit down, Vitelli. Your lawyer wouldn't have time to get here now. Besides, I think we won't question Rosa any further." He added abruptly:

"Gentlemen, I want you all to listen to me very carefully. And you two also, Rosa and Georgio. You, Rosa! You think we know nothing about this except what you've told us, don't you? Well, you're mistaken. We know a great deal about it." A grim smile pulled at the Doctor's lips.

"This is the New York Scientific Club—you know that. You were both born in New York—you're both intelligent enough to know what science is—what it can do. We brought you here, Rosa Vitelli, to *show you* with your own eyes how you killed Angelina Torno.

"We guessed how you did it—Sergeant Marberry guessed it—but it was only a guess. Not proof. Then, last week, we of the Scientific Club—using apparatus which you will see working in a moment—we *proved* it. Ah! That interests you, Rosa?

"Well, you watch and you will see." His tone grew ironical. "If we show you anything wrong, you can tell us." He whirled on Georgio.

"You, Vitelli, you'd better watch closely also. You'll want to repeat it all to your wife's lawyer. By the way, gentlemen, I have not yet told you that Rosa Vitelli's father is a fairly wealthy contractor down on Staten Island. He has retained quite able counsel to defend his daughter."

The Vitellis sat silent under this swift tirade. Several of the club members were murmuring to each other and the Doctor raised his hand for silence.

3

"YOU GENTLEMEN WILL be interested in this demonstration. It involves a well known scientific principle which only recently has been brought to its present practical perfection. Professor Walton here—" the Doctor indicated a frail, gray-haired man who sat apart with the excited Very Young Man—"Professor Walton has perfected an apparatus which he and Jack Bruce are shortly to operate for us—and which will show Rosa Vitelli in the very act of murdering Angelina Torno.

"Sit down, Rosa! We're not going to hurt you. No, Vitelli, you don't need the lawyer—you can tell him all about it."

The Doctor gazed over the room and, when he resumed, his tone was quieter.

"Gentlemen, the scientific principle involved is that of light rays. Light, as you know, is a vibration—of the ether let us say for convenience. A vibration which travels at the rate of one hundred and eighty-six thousand three hundred and twenty-four miles a second.

"A little boy once asked me a very naïve question which I am going to ask you gentlemen. He demanded of me: 'Dr. Adams, where does light go when it goes *out?*' You need not smile—I am quite serious." The Doctor was watching Rosa narrowly without appearing to do so.

A few of the club members had smiled, but Rosa and

her husband sat stolid—the young Italian listening intently and with apparent intelligence to the Doctor's words; and Rosa staring sullenly at the floor.

"I repeat that, gentlemen. Where does light go when it goes out? Let me show you something." He signaled to the Very Young Man who produced a candle and placed it upright on the center table. Rosa turned to face it, staring fascinated while the Very Young Man lighted it.

"Now, Jack."

The Very Young Man switched off the center electrolier; the room was plunged into gloom—flickering yellow candle light which disclosed little more than the table-top and the Doctor's standing figure.

The Doctor went on: "Light rays from this candle are bringing the image of it to your eyes at the rate of 186,000 miles a second. An inconceivable velocity measured over so short a distance. You see my hand reaching toward the candle? I touch it with my finger—so. Now, gentlemen, understand me. You did not see me touch that candle at the *exact* instant I actually touched it. There was a tiny interval of time in between—the time it took those light rays to carry the image ten or fifteen feet.

"Is that clear? I assure you it has a bearing upon the murder of Angelina Torno! I perform an act in this candle light; I touch the candle—so. And a tiny fraction of a second *after* I touch it, you see me touch it. A very tiny fraction of a second over such a short distance. But suppose you are ten times as far away, it will then be a tenfold greater interval of time.

"Then assume that you are on the moon, with a telescope powerful enough to observe me. I put a finger on the candle, and it is well over a second later that you see me do it. On the sun, some eight or nine minutes would have elapsed.

"On the nearest of the fixed stars you would not see my action until more than four years after I performed it. And observing me from one of the more distant stars, you would have to wait several hundred years!

"To go back to the child's question—watch my hand now, snuffing out the candle." The Doctor pinched out the wick; the room was black. Amid a shuffling of feet and a startled cry from Rosa, the Doctor's voice cried, "Lights, Jack!"

The lights flashed on. The Doctor resumed quietly: "You saw me snuff the candle. Those light rays brought the image to you at that tremendous velocity. They went on past you. Where? Out! Quite so. But not obliterated, gentlemen. Not lost. Remember that, for it is important. We are accustomed to a mode of reasoning which says that my act of snuffing that candle is *in the past,* dead and irrevocably gone. Not so!

"If you were watching me from the sun, at this present moment you would observe the candle still lighted and several minutes yet to wait before you would see me snuff it! To an observer on the sun, therefore, that particular act *has not yet been performed.* It is not in the past, but in the future.

"Do I make myself entirely clear? What I'm getting at, specifically, is this. The visual representation of every act ever performed is in existence at this present moment. Light does not go out—in the sense of being destroyed. It goes away.

"The light-rays that shone upon the white sands of San Salvador when Columbus knelt there, have not yet reached some of the distant stars. If you were on one of those stars, mechanically equipped to receive that image upon the retina of your eye, you could watch tonight and see Columbus discovering America!

"Thus no act can be accurately termed *of the past*, without reference to the equipment of the observer. Let me be still more specific. We think of the murder of Angelina Torno as an act of the past. It is not.

"If we could equip ourselves to receive the light rays carrying it. I said light rays did not go out, but away. They do that—but they also come back. Reflected light. Rosa, are you listening to all this?"

The girl raised her eyes from the floor. "Yes," she said sullenly. "I kill Angelina. Why you bother about me? I kill her, I tol' you."

"Yes," agreed the Doctor. "But I want you to listen and in a moment, watch closely what we're going to show you." He flashed a look at the young husband. "You're listening too, Vitelli?"

"Yes, I listen, but—"

"But you don't make much out of it?"

"No. Rosa's lawyer, he—"

"You can tell him," the Doctor interrupted. "You'll have a lot to tell him before we're finished. I was speaking of reflected light, gentlemen. It is reflected everywhere. Sunlight goes to the moon, and is reflected back to the earth. Our own light—itself mainly sunlight—goes to the moon and comes back to us again—and we call it moonlight.

"And here on earth, light is everywhere reflected back and forth. From the ceiling to the floor of this very room—from each of its walls to the other. Reflected constantly back and forth, like the reverberating echoes of sound."

4

THE DOCTOR PAUSED momentarily, then resumed. "I come now to the crux of the whole matter. Light rays, you must realize, are never lost. Their velocity never changes. Nor do they in their entirety, necessarily leave the neighborhood of their source.

"The sound of my voice—also vibrations which travel at something more than a thousand feet a second—will echo back and forth across this room for theoretically a limitless period. Growing dimmer—yes. Almost instantly, far below the very narrow range of our human hearing.

"And so it is with light vibrations. The light vibrations that candle sent out are still reverberating across this room. Altered in form. Dimmer—yes. Almost instantly far below the narrow range of our human sight. But, gentlemen, they are still here. And we could still see that candle being snuffed if we could isolate those light vibrations and again make them visible!"

There was no one who spoke when the Doctor halted. Rosa still kept her gaze on the floor. But though the girl's mentality could not follow the Doctor's reasoning, Georgio evidently understood to what this scientific analysis might lead. He gazed at his wife with an obvious, growing fear, and then back to the Doctor, as though fascinated.

The Doctor continued: "In principle, gentlemen, I have

told you it all. Some of you even, are familiar with the detailed workings of Professor Walton's apparatus. To the rest of you I need only add that he has succeeded—crudely, still with much to perfect—in isolating and magnifying let me say, otherwise invisible light vibrations. The modern radio does something of the kind with otherwise inaudible vibration of sound.

"To use popular language, Professor Walton 'tunes back' amid the mingled vibrations of light until he has isolated those he is seeking. They become crudely visible. The past, in so far as that particular scene is concerned, becomes the present."

The Doctor's voice rose to sudden vehemence. "In that tenement building where Angelina Torno lived, there are still vibrations of light carrying the scene of the murder. Professor Walton's apparatus is connected at this moment, with that building. Gentlemen, you are about to witness— not a representation of the murder—but the actual murder itself!"

As though his words were a signal, the Very Young Man without warning switched off the electrolier. The room went black. For a second or two only, and then a purple beam of light sprang from an unnoticed orifice in the wall. It bathed the room in its deep, lurid glare.

The thing was startling. Rosa screamed. Georgio was on his feet, but the detective pulled him back to his chair. Over the confusion the Doctor's voice sounded.

"Quiet, gentlemen. We did not mean to startle you."

The Very Young Man, sprung suddenly into action, was lowering a cord. Professor Walton hurried past him—and, unnoticed in the purple glare, went through a side door and out of the room. The cord which the Very Young Man was operating, lowered from the ceiling a shimmering veil—a rectangle some ten feet wide and eight feet high. It hung from the ceiling almost to the floor.

The occupants of the room all turned to face it. The purple beam of light from the wall orifice struck it from behind. It glowed—purple, then dissolving into scarlet: a blood-red veil, still quivering from the movement of its descent.

The Doctor's voice said: "The fabric of that veil is finely woven wire. The light is from Professor Walton's apparatus in the adjoining room. Vitelli, I want you to watch closely. Your lawyer will be interested in this. You, Rosa! You hear me? You watch this! I am going to show you yourself, in the very act of murdering Angelina Torno!"

A silence fell over the room. The club members, the Vitellis, the detective and assistant district attorney and the two policemen—all staring with a silent, awed fascination. The veil, blood-red, was creeping and crawling with color. Spots of shadow seemed forming upon it. Vague, distorted—formless blurs of movement, shifting slowly as a cloud bank—shapes dissolving formlessly one into the other.

A hum now filled the room. Low at first, then louder—a penetrating electrical hum. The Doctor raised his voice above it.

"Those blurs which you see are scenes in the third-floor hallway of the tenement building in question. Professor Walton's observing station is erected there. To the left is the door to the Vitelli flat. Angelina's door is directly across the hall to the right. Formless blurs, gentlemen, as yet.

"But wait a moment. Professor Walton is 'tuning back,' so to speak. Back through the mingled light vibrations until he reaches those of the murder scene. Watch, Rosa! Soon you will see!"

No need for his admonition. In the glare of red light the girl's figure showed as she sat in her chair, staring at the blood-red veil. The shadows there grew denser. Moving shapes—condensing, taking form.

The hum in the room went up an ascending scale, then struck a level. Like an accelerating dynamo, reaching its pitch and holding it. The Doctor spoke louder.

"Now! You see? We are back to the morning after the murder."

The blurred outlines of a tenement hallway became visible. To the left a wooden door—old-fashioned, dingy, with a glass transom above it. To the right, a similar-door. A dingy flight of stairs in the background, leading upward. In the center, depending from the low ceiling, a ramshackle chandelier. On the floor, worn, ragged oilcloth.

People—half a dozen men in uniform—Detective Marberry—moved about the scene—opened Angelina's door to the right—entered and emerged. The whole a deep crimson. Blurred, occasionally grotesquely distorted; then again clearly distinguishable.

"The morning after the murder," the Doctor repeated. "Imperfect—as imperfect an apparatus as were our first, unimproved radios. And now—look, Rosa! Now we are going back to the murder itself!"

The crimson scene blurred again into formless crawling patches of light and shade. The hum slid upward to still a higher pitch; held even and the blurs clarified. The hallway again. Empty and dark—so dark that only the stairs and the dim outlines of the doors left and right, were visible. An empty, motionless scene. Sinister, expectant.

And then, very slowly, the left-hand door was opening. There was no light behind it; only a dark rectangle of shadow there. Then a flare. A pencil-point of light showed—moved—came out of the doorway; resolved itself into a human hand holding a lighted candle.

For a moment nothing else in the blood-red gloom was visible. The hand with the candle advanced slowly into the center of the hallway. And now a dim blur of human shape beside it seemed almost distinguishable.

The hand with the candle stopped. The candle-light seemed unnaturally to disclose nothing. Then the other hand appeared—a hand reaching upward, holding a long rubber pipe of the sort used to connect small gas heaters. The hand slipped the rubber pipe over the hallway gas-jet; fumbled there, then moved away; carrying the other end of the pipe to the transom above Angelina's door; pushing the transom open cautiously; sticking the pipe-end through, and closing the transom close upon it.

All blurred, dark-red, and barely distinguishable. Swiftly done; a few seconds only. And then abruptly the scene brightened and clarified further. The outlines of the figure adjusting the pipe—turning on the gas—suddenly became plainly visible. Not a woman's figure! Not Rose Vitelli. The figure of a tall, slender, dark-haired man. Georgio Vitelli! Unmistakable!

5

IT WAS SO abruptly disclosed that a gasp ran over the onlookers. The hum ceased. The blood-light went out. From the black darkness of the clubroom came the sounds of scuffling feet; an outcry from Rosa—her terrified, despairing moan in Italian: "They know I did not do it! Georgio! Beloved! Run! Run! Run!"

Her wild burst of sobbing; pattering footsteps; the clatter of a chair overturned; a thump; a body falling; an oath from the Very Young Man, and then his voice rising above the tumult:

"Light the lights! I've got him! Light the lights, somebody! I tell you I've got him!"

The lights flashed on. Rosa sat in her chair, sobbing. On the floor by the door lay the struggling form of Georgio Vitelli with the muscular Very Young Man upon him.

The detective leaped to Rosa, gripping her by the shoulders, shaking her. "You saw that, Rosa! Why did you tell us you killed Angelina? You didn't kill her!"

"No! No!"

Still shaking her. "Why did you say you did? Why?"

"My Georgio—he—he tol' me to say I did it."

She was sobbing, oblivious to what was going on around her. The assistant district attorney rushed up to them. The detective shook the girl again.

"He told you to confess! Why? Why did you do it?"

"He tol' me to say I did it—because I'm a girl. I get off. He tol' me that. And you—you try always to make me to say how I kill Angelina." She broke into an hysterical flood of Italian. The detective released her. He said swiftly:

"As we thought. Says she never knew how or why her husband killed Angelina. She didn't know how it was done, so of course she couldn't tell us. It's obvious that he was afraid to let her know—afraid she might be clumsy and say something that would arouse our suspicions—incriminate him. Is *he* talking? Now's the psychological moment—we must *make* him talk!"

But the Very Young Man had already made Vitelli talk. Cuffed him on the head, choked him—until the Doctor and others pulled them apart. And in the confusion, hearing Rosa blurt out the truth and before he could gather his wits, Vitelli had confessed.

When the room had quieted, with Vitelli in charge of the two policemen and Rosa still sobbing softly to herself, the Doctor spoke.

"We have been successful, gentlemen—and I think that you probably understand almost everything which has transpired. Professor Walton would have me tell you that in fundamental principle every theory of light which I gave you is quite correct. Indeed, it is a hope of his that someday an apparatus such as I described will be perfected.

"But for our ignorant present, we had to use a motion picture. That was what you saw, gentlemen. A purposely crude and jumbled motion picture tinted red, made a few days ago with a young Italian actor playing the part of

Vitelli. The scene so blurred and dark, it was easy to catch the likeness.

"For the crime itself: Sergeant Marberry unearthed that newspaper clipping. I chanced to see it myself the day it was published. A rubber tube was discovered in a hallway, a tube leading gas from the hallway jet through a transom into a flat. A whole family narrowly escaped asphyxiation. No motive, no criminal was located—and the thing went by the board.

"But it gave Vitelli his inspiration—and reading it, Sergeant Marberry saw at once that the Torno girl could have been murdered in similar fashion.

"Other facts which Marberry brought to light, made that assumption still more probable. The gas-jet in the hallway on the Vitelli-Torno floor was *lighted* the night before; and in the morning the janitor found it turned out. Also: On the oilcloth floor of the hallway, Marberry found drippings of red wax. They suggested that a candle had been used by the criminal to furnish light. Red wax.

"Perhaps one of those small Christmas candles of which the Italians are so fond. And it was only a few weeks after Christmas. As a matter of fact, the stump of a red-wax Christmas candle was found in the Vitelli kitchen.

"Another fact. Above the Vitellis, the tenants smelled a peculiar burning smell that night. Burning rubber! They recognized it at once. We knew then that the gas tube had probably been burned in the Vitelli grate—and now Rosa tells us this moment that her husband did burn something in the grate that night, and would not let her know what it was. This grate, by the way, is an unique feature of the Vitelli flat—the only grate in the whole building.

"All this indicated to us that either one, or perhaps both of the Vitellis, was guilty. Especially in view of their turbulent relations with Angelina. Then, before any of the evidence had been used against them, Rosa confessed. It is obvious now that Georgio soon realized that one or both of them would be arrested. And so he made her confess, to save himself. And she obviously loved him little short of idolatry.

"To us, even then, it seemed a dubious confession for two reasons. First: Rosa would not tell how she committed the murder. Her lawyer soon counseled silence; but in the first hysteria when she confessed, we were convinced that she had no such counsel. And her response to questions was such, that we felt right along she had no knowledge of how gas was introduced into that flat. We made several cautious tests. For instance, to the sudden smell of burning rubber Rosa reacted much more innocently than did her husband.

"Our second reason for doubting the truth of Rosa's confession: The murdered girl was to become a mother. That changed the whole complexion of the affair, gentlemen! The probability was that Rosa did not know of this— but that Giorgio did. It supplied a very strong motive for him to kill this other girl who had suddenly become a millstone about his neck. Especially since, only two days before the murder, Rosa's father, thinking to straighten out his daughter's marital difficulties, offered Giorgio an excellent position in his contracting business, and insisted that the young couple move to Staten Island near him. Giorgio accepted. But Angelina had undoubtedly become a menace—and so h killed her.

"All this we could reason out. But with Rosa confess-

ing to the murder—and in the hands of able counsel—
what could Mr. Green do? Nothing, but what we did here
tonight.

"Rosa's motive for the confession? Self-sacrifice, gentlemen. She loved her husband—still does. And he told her
to confess. Doubtless pictured how Angelina had ensnared
him—how, if caught, *he* would go to the electric chair. And
assured her that a young, pretty wife, murdering a rival for
jealousy, would get a very light sentence, if any. And true
enough. Especially in Italian cases. Courts are very sympathetic with the perfectly natural trait of violent, passionate
jealousy in a pretty, young Italian girl. And most especially
if she can prove she had cause to be jealous, and confesses
at once to her crime. The District Attorney has had that
sort of thing to fight before. It made this case extremely
awkward. And Vitelli—guilty, undoubtedly, of first degree
murder—would go scot-free."

The Doctor paused, and on an impulse went to the still
sobbing Rosa and bent over her. "Your father will be very
pleased, Rosa," he said gently. "You see—though you don't
realize it now—your Giorgio isn't worth all these tears."
He patted her shoulder and turned back to the room. "Poor
little child! Only eighteen—and to have had a start in life
like this!"

POISONED HARMONY

"**IT IS ONE** of those attempts at a bizarre crime," said the Doctor. "So bizarre, in fact, that it was foredoomed to failure."

He smiled at the detective by his side and then at the interested group of club members dispersed about the small clubroom. "Foredoomed to failure, gentlemen. Sergeant Marberry will tell you that the more bizarre and unusual a crime is, the less chance it has of success."

The detective nodded. "I have found that generally the case, Dr. Adams. The extremely simple crime, almost devoid of details, is by far more difficult to—"

"Did you get us here to listen to an abstract argument on crime?" testily demanded the Banker.

The Very Young Man spoke up diffidently. "Dr. Adams, you said there were two crimes. Shouldn't you explain that they were both committed by—"

"Two attempts at murder," the Doctor corrected. "Both extremely unusual attempts—both unsuccessful—" He turned smilingly to the Banker. "You're impatient, George? Very well. To be specific, then, our problem is this: Someone has made two successive attempts at murder. Who is guilty? That we cannot tell.

"We can guess—but that isn't enough. Sergeant Marberry is afraid he would never be able to prove anything by ordinary methods. And he had an idea which we might use here in the Scientific Club—"

The Alienist interrupted. "You'd better outline the case, Frank. I, for one, know nothing of it at all. Rogers does, I can see that." His gesture indicated the Chemist. "But you haven't taken me into your confidence. You say, two attempts at murder, both obviously made by the same person against the same person? Is that it? One case, not two?"

"Exactly," said the Doctor. "The outward circumstances, gentlemen, are briefly these. It appears that someone is trying to murder a very famous man. Most of you have heard of Vladimir Polman, no doubt, the concert pianist. He is a man now of sixty-odd—possibly he has reached seventy. Of Central European birth, naturalized American, and he has made his home here in America for the past twenty years.

"As a pianist, he has ranked among the best. You heard him at Carnegie Hall, some of you, a month ago. He is— well, between ourselves, somewhat *passé* now. But he clings on—and no doubt we should admire him for it.

"He is a queer, dogged old man—a genius unquestionably. A player like Franz Liszt, who, he says, was greatest of them all. For myself, I disagree. I don't like that showy, fireworks sort of playing. Liszt must have been like that— certainly Polman is. He—"

"Did you get us here to listen to a musical argument?" the Banker inquired sarcastically. "What do I care about Franz Liszt?"

"Nothing, George, no doubt. But I'm discussing Polman. At all events, Sergeant Marberry recently was called to the Polman home here in New York, when an attempt upon the pianist's life was accidentally discovered. Polman's study is on the top floor of the house. His grand piano is there—and the room by its isolation makes possible his undisturbed practice.

"On the evening in question, it seems that Polman's little daughter—she is six years old—wandered into his study when it was unoccupied. She stood by the piano, as a child will, and strummed—pounded—upon the keys. It was at about eight o'clock. The family were all downstairs just finishing dinner—the child was supposed to be upstairs in bed asleep.

"The little girl had left the study door open when she entered. Downstairs, the family heard the sudden sharp crack of a revolver shot. Rushing up, they found the child standing by the piano crying with terror. The smell of the powder was still in the room.

"There was no sign of an intruder. The windows were all closed and locked. Somewhere from within the room a shot had been fired. But not at the child, gentlemen. She was standing at the left end of the piano beside the bass keys, strumming them.

"The bullet missed her, for it went directly over the center of the bench, striking the front face of the piano above middle C. Polman notified the police at once, and the family waited there in the room, disturbing nothing, until Sergeant Marberry arrived very soon after."

The Doctor paused momentarily. "We have no wish to mystify you, gentlemen. A moment's thought will show you that it was obvious under the circumstances that the weapon had not been discharged by a human hand. It was

An instant of breathless silence; then the fingers moved.

fired from within the room, from a point sufficiently close so that, had the little girl been its mark, she would have been hit, or at least not missed by so great a margin.

"The point at which the bullet struck was also significant. Obviously had Polman been seated at the piano, playing, the bullet would have entered his back and pierced his heart. So before Sergeant Marberry had been there five minutes, he was convinced that the weapon had been mechanically discharged. A search of the room, in fact, revealed it. I have it here—Jack, let me have it, will you?"

There was a stir in the clubroom as the Very Young Man produced a wooden container about the size and shape of a shoe box, and handed it to the Doctor.

"The box itself is of our own making," the Doctor explained. "What Marberry found—hidden behind the curtain of a bookcase across Polman's study—was this." He drew from the box a small wooden frame into which a revolver was clamped. The weapon was held in a horizontal position.

To its trigger was fastened a small but powerful spring,

stretched to full tension. There was a slender white rod beside the spring, holding the trigger rigid. A simple but mysterious-looking contrivance, crudely fashioned, yet businesslike and distinctly sinister.

The Doctor placed it on the table. "Before I explain this, gentlemen—and I repeat, there is nothing inexplicable about it—I think I should tell you something of the possible motives for the crime. The weapon itself is simple enough. But who made it, and set it like a trap ready to spring upon its victim? There is our problem. There were no fingerprints. Where the revolver was obtained we do not know.

"But there are some things we do know. For instance, we are convinced—for reasons which you will shortly understand—that some member of the Polman household is guilty. It is obviously, as they say, an inside job.

"The Polman household consists of old Vladimir Polman, his young second wife, their one child—the little girl I have already mentioned—and an adopted son—Alan Polman. Of the servants, there is only one of importance—a Mrs. Rance, the housekeeper."

"I've heard of Alan Polman," the Astronomer interjected.

"Yes. Of course you have. Gentlemen, I will be very brief with the family history—yet it is necessary. Vladimir Polman and his first wife—a Polish woman—were childless. In England—twenty-three years ago—they adopted a three-year-old orphan.

"He is this Alan Polman. His parents were both obscure musicians, which is why the Polmans selected him. They trained him in music and he showed signs of genius. And

today, at twenty-six, he has almost a national fame as a
pianist. Indeed, just between ourselves, he is as great an
artist as his foster father.

"Ten years ago Polman's first wife died. Three years later
he married his present wife. She was an actress in musical
comedy, which she promptly gave up. A year later, this little
girl was born to them. So much for the family. The housekeeper, Mrs. Rance, has been with them some twelve years.
She is mentioned for a considerable legacy in Polman's will;
and she has a son in college."

"Polman's will," exclaimed the Lawyer. "There you have
the crux of the matter."

"Possibly," said the Doctor. "Polman is a wealthy man.
His will, which was made shortly after his second marriage,
seems quite reasonable. A substantial legacy—I believe it
is twenty thousand dollars—to the housekeeper. The rest
of the estate—something over a million—divided about
equally between his wife and the adopted son."

"Rather a large share for an adopted son," the Lawyer
commented.

"Yes—the wife might think so—I do not believe, gentlemen, that we need theorize on motives too closely. Vladimir Polman is not really old—he may conceivably live ten
or fifteen years more—he is in very good physical condition. And when you have three heirs of a wealthy man,
none of whom have any great reason to love him, the possible motive for each of them is about the same."

"Tell them about Alan Polman," the Very Young Man
interjected eagerly. "The evidence—"

2

"ALAN POLMAN," SAID the Doctor, "has perhaps the greatest motive. He may be artistically the equal of the old man, but our public has not yet fully recognized him. He is gaining in reputation very fast, but still his earnings, compared to Polman Senior, are very small."

"This contrivance here on the table," the Banker interrupted. "Why don't you show us how it works? I don't care about—"

The clubroom door opened and an attendant announced, "Mr. Vladimir Polman and family to see Dr. Adams."

The visitors were upon the threshold. The Very Young Man hastily replaced the revolver and its mechanism in the box and got it out of sight.

The visitors entered, and for a moment the room was a confusion of introductions. There were five of the newcomers. Vladimir Polman—tall, spare, an erect, muscular figure in his frock coat and flowing black tie, a musician of the old school: smooth-shaven with a rugged, strong face, thin-lipped; gray eyes beneath shaggy eyebrows; a huge mole on his forehead; a great mane of shaggy white hair. A dominant personality—erratic, dogmatic in all his ideas and opinions. A genius.

Beside him, as the Doctor found them chairs, was his wife—a plump, pretty woman in her thirties, lavishly dressed, heavily perfumed. A rosebud mouth; a face like a doll, save for its keen, calculating eyes; a woman with the luster of wealth upon her, wrapped in the dignity of her position, and yet who just missed being a lady.

At her mother's side stood the little girl, with the house-keeper—a thin, drab, but competent-looking woman—seated nearby.

The fifth of the visitors sat somewhat apart. At first glance, most of the club members would have said that they liked Alan Polman. At twenty-six, he looked considerably younger—no more than a boy—a fact doubtless brought about by his years of playing as a child prodigy.

A tall, very slender figure; a handsome, clean-shaven face, pale and studious. Lips slightly sensuous—a mouth like that of a pretty girl. But a strong, masculine jaw, deep-set blue eyes, and thick wavy brown hair, worn just a trifle long. A pleasant, ready smile—but at the moment it seemed forced. Obviously he was ill at ease, though as he took his seat he met the detective's glance and nodded smilingly.

After an interval of conversation aside with the detective and the Very Young Man, the Doctor addressed them in general.

"I have asked you all to come here," he began quietly, "hoping that we may be able to shed some light upon the attempt recently made to murder Mr. Polman. Sergeant Marberry told you of Mr. Polman's household, that he was going to drop the matter. His plans changed. It is not going to be dropped." He waited for some comment, but none came.

"And now that we are all here," he continued, "with these

few members of the club for witnesses, I am not going to mince words. I want to tell you of Mr. Polman's household, that we feel very strongly that one of you here now in this room has attempted a murder."

It was a quiet, but firm statement. The visitors seemed surprised and perturbed. They stared at each other questioningly.

Mrs. Polman murmured, "How dare you!" with dignity; the housekeeper whitened and set her lips firmly, seeming to shrink into her chair. Alan was merely solemn, gazing steadily at the Doctor, but seeming to hold himself tense.

"A potential murderer among you," the Doctor repeated. "And I am sure that all of you—save one—would want us to find out who it is."

The Doctor exchanged a meaning glance with Polman Senior, who sat grimly listening to the proceedings; then the Doctor added with a note of menace in his tone:

"I am going to use no finesse or evasion. In a word, gentlemen, the further evidence which I will present to you in a moment points very strongly to this young man here—Alan Polman."

The words visibly surprised most of the club members. But Alan still held himself firm, returning the Doctor's accusing gaze, but making no move to speak. The Doctor added quickly: "Jack, let me have that box."

The revolver with its mechanism was placed on the table. The Polman family had all seen it before; they regarded it now with fascinated stares.

"This," continued the Doctor, "was contrived as the murder weapon. Someone rigged it up, and placed it where a bullet from it would pierce the heart of Mr. Polman as he sat at his piano. I said, gentlemen, that we feel this to be an inside job. Here is the reason.

"Alan Polman is more than a musician. An amateur scientist—he has a very keen interest in it. For some years past he has hoped to invent a—shall I say—phonetic typewriter. One into which you can speak, and it will be operated by the voice vibrations. He has, indeed, a well equipped little laboratory in his foster father's home, where for some time he has been testing—"

The Banker tried to interrupt, but the Doctor silenced him. "Just a moment, George. This is all very important, for it was in Alan's laboratory that the vital material for this murder weapon was made. The materials are all there—"

The Lawyer spoke up. "May I ask a few pertinent questions?"

"Certainly," agreed the Doctor.

"Alan Polman, you say, had at hand all the materials necessary for the construction of this murder weapon?"

"Yes."

"And the scientific knowledge to construct it?"

"Undoubtedly."

"How about these other members of the household?"

"We do not know what their scientific knowledge is, but usually a woman isn't—"

"You say the scientific principle involved is simple?"

"Yes. Unusual perhaps, but perfectly simple."

"It was a principle involved in this typewriter invention of Alan's?"

"Yes."

"Then hearing him discuss it about the household, might not these women pick it up—and easily understand it?"

The Doctor hesitated. "Yes—I suppose so."

"The household had free access to the laboratory?"

"Yes. So I understand. They did not go in it very often—Alan did not encourage them to."

"But it was not locked?"

"No."

"Then they had access." The Lawyer thought a moment. "This housekeeper—you say she has a son in college?"

"Yes."

The housekeeper was visibly perturbed. She attempted to protest, but the Doctor silenced her. The Lawyer went on:

"This son—he might perhaps be taking a scientific course. Is he?"

"No," said the housekeeper. "I—perhaps he is. Really, I'm not sure. But he—"

"Was he in the Polman home at the time of this attempted murder?" the Lawyer persisted.

"No," the Doctor answered. "Not for some two weeks before."

"I see." The Lawyer turned suddenly to Mrs. Polman. "Were *you* interested in Alan's scientific work?"

The woman was surprised, but after a momentary flush, she said evenly: "Your inference is insulting. I did not come here to be cross-examined."

"You refuse to answer?"

"Yes. I consider the question none of your business."

The Lawyer smiled blandly. "Possibly you are right."

There was a pause.

"Is that all?" the Doctor asked.

The Lawyer had relaxed in his chair. "Yes—thanks."

The Doctor went on: "Alan Polman denies all knowledge of the affair, gentlemen. Innocent or guilty, we have no proof."

Innocent or guilty? No one in the room could have told, as they regarded the young musician. He sat perfectly quiet, solemn, and pale.

"I want to know how that revolver works," the Banker declared out of a silence.

"You shall know at once," the Doctor said readily. "There is only one other fact I want to mention. The Polman piano which received the bullet, and at which the murder was planned to take place, has been repaired. I would have it here this afternoon, but it is in another part of the club. As most of you know, Mr. Polman Senior is giving us a benefit concert here this evening.

"Both he and Alan are to play, and the piano—which, as you have doubtless read, is the only one Mr. Polman will play upon in public—is upstairs now in our little concert hall. I have a piano here, however, which will serve equally as well for our demonstration of how the murder weapon is operated."

The Doctor indicated a small upright piano which stood across the room against the wall. Then he gestured toward the contrivance on the table before him.

3

—

"**THE WAY IN** which this revolver was planned to fire is what interests us now. I will ask you all to listen close-ly—a very simple and perfectly understandable scientific principle—"

He seemed to be watching the two women closely. The Astronomer noticed it, for he whispered to the Very Young Man:

"He's trying to find out how much those women know of science."

The Very Young Man's answering whisper was tense. "Wait! It's that second murder attempt he's after. Watch him!"

"—perfectly understandable principle," the Doctor was saying. "You have all reasoned, of course, that it was this child's chance pounding upon the piano which fired the revolver. Quite so. It was set and aimed to strike the heart of a player seated in the normal position before the keyboard—and so it missed the child. It was fired, gentle-men, by certain vibrations of the piano strings.

"I say, 'certain vibrations.' Let me illustrate. Music we call an art. But it is a science as well—the science of pleasing vibrations of sound. I'm not going to weary you with its intricacies. The timbre—tone quality, for instance—is that which makes a violin sound different from a piano, even though both play the identical note. That is a question of overtones and many other factors. We are concerned only with the fundamental vibrations of the string—vibrations which by their frequency determine the pitch."

He rose to his feet, and propped a book partly under the base of the revolver frame so that its muzzle pointed diagonally upward toward the ceiling.

"This revolver is not loaded. But lest the ladies are fearful of it, I aim it harmlessly upward."

He went to the piano as he spoke. A tenseness fell over the spectators. The room was dead silent, with all eyes upon the revolver as it stood there on the table.

The Doctor continued quietly: "Vibrations will fire that weapon, but not all vibrations. It would not have been very practical if any vibration at all would set it off. I clap my hands—so. You observe that the trigger was not pulled by the spring. I stamp the floor—" His foot clapped the polished wooden surface.

"Nothing happens. As for the mechanism itself, you can all see it from where you are sitting. The spring is at full tension. If free to act, it would pull the trigger. But you observe, there is a very slender, rigid rod connecting the base of the spring, where it fastened to the frame, with the trigger. A rigid rod, gentlemen, holding the trigger against the pull of the spring.

"A fragile rod. It looks like glass. It is not just that—but something akin to it—an ingenious substance perfected by Alan Polman for use in his invention. It is under considerable strain—that slender rod—holding the pull of the spring. If it shatters, the spring will recoil and pull the trigger.

"But the rod will not shatter from any ordinary vibration. For its length, diameter and the strain upon it—all carefully calculated—it will vibrate and break only in response to one particular vibration—and that reiterated a number of times.

"Have you ever had a metal ornament on a piano or near it, and been annoyed by its vibration in response to one particular note on the instrument? This is something like that. But this needs the cumulative effect of reiteration. I remember once being in the New York Hippodrome and watching an enormous troupe of Maori dancers. They had a curious barefoot dance—a stamping of feet upon the wooden stage.

"A hundred or two of them stamping together. It reverberated throughout that vast auditorium—rhythmic, absolutely unchanged for some five minutes. Slowly the building began to vibrate with it. The seat under me, literally trembling; the whole span of the balcony on which I was sitting seeming to shudder in response to that rhythmic vibration from the stage.

"I remembered that Marconi had once said that if he were to use the right vibration, however small in itself, reiterated often enough, he could shatter with it all the office buildings in Manhattan. And when those Maoris stopped dancing, I was actually tremendously relieved."

The Doctor's smile faded as he went on: "The ingenious part of this case, my friends, is that no ordinary use of the piano will fire that revolver. Only one note of the keyboard, played over and over, will accomplish it. Yet, the would-be murderer knew that there is a musical composition which would do just that—and it is a well-known piece which is in Mr, Polman's répertoire and which he is frequently in the habit of practicing."

The Doctor strummed the piano keys. "I have had this piano tuned to the exact pitch of Mr. Polman's. You notice—I reiterate, middle C. It has no effect. Nor has A—so. The note is G sharp. We found that out by actual test, Sergeant Marberry and myself. Any G sharp. They are all the same—an octave vibrates readily with its mates—each higher octave merely a doubling of the vibration frequency.

"Knowing it was G sharp, I happened upon the piece. My daughter plays it very well—and once you know its peculiarity, you never forget it. It is the Chopin 'Prelude in D Flat, Opus 28, No. 15,' to be exact—popularly known as 'The Raindrop.' There is an interesting little story about it—a dream Chopin had of a storm—dreaming of a tragedy—raindrops falling upon the dead faces of his children—his and George Sand.

"Something like that—a dream only, but the next day he composed this prelude. The story is immaterial. Enough to say that the prelude is built almost entirely upon a reiterated G sharp—the raindrops falling, woven into a pathetic little melody. Jack, let me have that music."

He opened up a thin volume of Chopin. "You see the G sharps? Pages of them. Scored as A flat under the first signature, but it's the same note, of course. Pages of it, reiterated from one end of the thing to the other.

"A queer circumstance, gentlemen, which no one but a musician—or of a musician's family—would be likely to know." He turned abruptly to the elder Polman. "Will you play this for us, Mr. Polman? I want these gentlemen to hear it—to observe its action upon that revolver."

The old musician was surprised. Then he assented, but he spurned the music. "I do not use music," he said with dignity. "But I will play it, if you wish." He went to the piano.

A silence as deep as any artist about to play could wish for, fell over the room as he took his seat. The Doctor stood tense. The Very Young Man whispered something to the man beside him, and was instantly rebuked. Many eyes were upon Alan Polman. He was pale and solemn as always, leaning forward, staring at the piano as though held by its fascination. Polman arranged his frock coat with the familiar public gesture that was his custom, swept a hand majestically through his shaggy hair, rested his fingers lightly upon the keyboard, stared dreamily before him: his familiar theatrical pose; but it was effective.

An instant of breathless silence; then the strong, slender fingers moved. A gentle, tender melody floated into the room, simple as a folk-song, infinitely sweet and pathetic. And woven into it—underlying it—a slow, reiterated tone.

The revolver clicked, sharp and clear in the silence; but it was scarcely noticed, for almost simultaneously the piano clashed a discord. Not caused by the revolver, but by Polman's elbow as it fell against the bass keys. He had twisted himself about, and was rising from the stool.

"You—you—"

Swaying, he stood facing the room, his face gone ashen. Eyes wild—terror thickening his tongue; his right hand gripping his hair, his left hand held dangling before him. And from the tip of one of his left hand fingers a tiny drop of blood was oozing out.

"You—you've killed me! So—you've killed me!"

The Doctor and the detective sprang at him. "Killed you? Killed you?"

A moment longer he stood, staring stupidly at the drop of blood on his finger. Then his terrified, hysterical cry rang out.

"Killed me! You know it! Both of you! All of you! I want a doctor! I—*you're* a doctor—you know what it is—this poison, as well as I do! The numbness creeping over me—I feel it now! Fools! You would stand there staring—"

They drew it from him then—his babbled confession. At the point of death, with the Doctor sternly refusing to minister to him—he told it all freely.

And then the Doctor said: "You need not worry, Mr. Polman. You are not going to die. That was merely a needle prick—perfectly harmless. Your man, Marberry."

He swung about and addressed the room. "Be seated, please—all of you. There is no harm done—if you will be seated, I shall gladly explain."

4

THE ROOM WAS restored to a semblance of order. In his chair, Polman was still babbling. Denying everything now—but it was useless, and presently the detective silenced him.

"From what I know of crime detection," the Doctor began, "most guilty witnesses, when under the fire of police questioning, are readily recognized. That is not the difficulty. It is in breaking them down—in proving them guilty. You'd be surprised, gentlemen, to realize how many cases are fully known in the District Attorney's office—and yet how they will stand up in court is problematical."

"This was such a case. Sergeant Marberry and his superior saw at once that the elder Polman possibly was guilty. Why the elder Polman? Because, curiously enough, although all the motives and circumstances went to prove that Alan had attempted to murder his foster father—the exact reverse was equally plausible.

"I refer now to the period shortly after the revolver episode. We at first suspected Alan. Polman openly accused him to us. We could prove nothing and pretended to drop the case. Then Alan came to us privately, with a very significant statement.

"The afternoon of the revolver episode, Polman had persuaded Alan to play 'The Raindrop' prelude publicly, instead of himself. He suggested that Alan brush up on it that evening—on Polman's piano, although always before Alan had used his own study and his own instrument. Mrs. Rance, the housekeeper, overheard this conversation and privately testified so, to us.

"We believed Alan—believed him mainly because the truth always has the ring of truth. He told us things about the old gentleman's attitude toward him—things we could realize were true, but never hoped to prove.

"Then came this forthcoming concert here in the club. Suspecting what we did, it seemed very significant that Polman should give us the program, the *first* number of which was 'The Raindrop' prelude, to be played by Alan Polman!

"Believing that we had dropped the matter entirely, Polman planned a second attempt to murder his adopted son. He had been almost successful in blaming the first one upon Alan, when it went awry, and so he grew bolder.

"A poisoned needle, gentlemen, inserted alongside the black key of G sharp. It would prick Alan's finger. In the absorption of a public recital, the slight hurt would never be noticed. Alan would finish his performance, be taken speedily and violently sick, and die. And the tiny prick as the cause of death would never be discovered.

"From Polman's viewpoint, he was never in great danger of being exposed. The revolver, had it killed Alan, would have appeared to be Alan's own attempt to murder his foster father, come as a boomerang upon himself.

"It would have been an accident—a premature firing of the weapon, while Alan was arranging it. A murderer caught in his own trap—so Polman planned to make it appear. Then, when that went awry, this needle, Polman hoped, would remain forever a mystery.

"But we found it—this morning when the Polman piano was delivered to the club. Mr. Polman, in his familiar dogmatic way, forbade anyone touching it in advance of the concert—he was not taking any chance of another accident, you see—and Alan was to play the first number.

"But we found the needle—for we made a thorough search of the piano, which was the only rational thing to do under the circumstances. Alan himself insisted on it. Knowing in his heart—as we could never know—that he was innocent, he was convinced that Polman was trying to murder him. And when we found the needle, we planned this affair here this afternoon.

"Polman's motive? To a man like himself, one of the strongest. And a little pathetic, gentlemen. He is an old man. *Passé* now. Seeing his own reputation going down and clinging to it, he watched this young namesake take his place. Youth, vitality—rising; and all the while his own forces slipping from him. Alan was not his own child, you remember. Love for the child he had adopted had slowly turned to hate through the years as the prodigy grew to manhood. The prodigy was something to be proud of—to smile down upon—to train and encourage. But the man was a rival. A new Polman, displacing the old all too soon. Winning Vladimir Polman's adoring public away from him. It grew unbearable.

"As I said before, gentlemen, these bizarre, unusual crimes, even when circumstances make them normal and easy to plan, are not generally difficult to detect. Polman undoubtedly thought himself very clever in planning so elaborate a crime—even down to the will made out less than a month ago. Doubtless he studied it, worked over it for weeks ahead. The preparation of the needle needed no particularly technical knowledge—but to procure the poison with safe secrecy must have taken a good deal of care."

The Doctor shrugged. "For myself, I'd rather make sure I had no spectators and then shove my victim off the dock. As Marberry will tell you, a simple murder like that is much more complicated to solve."

WHAT THOUGHT DID

"**BUT ARE YOU** convinced we are justified in mixing up in this thing?" the Banker objected.

"I think so. If that poor girl was murdered—"

The Banker interrupted, waving his hand toward the table with its littered pile of newspapers, around which the earnest men were sitting. "Nobody knows that she was murdered. You told us yourself that the papers say—"

"I said *if* she was murdered, George," the Doctor rejoined patiently. "That is what I propose to find out. My experiment certainly can do no harm, and it is quite in line with the interests of this club. If it is successful we shall have fastened the guilt upon one of these unfortunate young men and cleared the other. If not—" He shrugged. "Well, then the police can proceed as they are now doing."

"I agree with Dr. Adams," spoke up the Chemist. "One of these two young men possibly is a murderer—at large in the community. If Dr. Adams believes that simply by summoning them to this room he can determine which is which, he should do so."

A chorus of affirmation came from the men. The Doctor said quietly: "I have taken the liberty of sending for them. They will be here very shortly."

"You seem to have studied the case, Frank," said the Big

Business Man. "Why not give us the main facts. I, for one, haven't read it at all."

The Doctor nodded. "The case is extraordinarily meager of detail, gentlemen. And I think its very simplicity argues strongly that it can never be solved by ordinary methods. Maple Grove, as you know, is one of the Jersey suburbs of New York City. A year ago there came to Maple Grove two brothers—Robert and James Blake—at that time twenty-four and twenty-six years old respectively.

"Nothing is known of them beyond the fact that they were without much money, and have since been working— both of them—in the factory of the Tonola Phonograph Company. They state that they are orphans, of English descent, without relatives in this country.

"Robert Blake—the younger—two months ago married rather suddenly, Edith Van Loan—to quote the newspapers, 'the charming daughter of R. V. Van Loan, millionaire leather manufacturer'—the Van Loan estate is the show place of Maple Grove. James Blake was also in love with the girl—his brother's unsuccessful rival. The young couple lived in a small bungalow near the Van Loan mansion— bought for them by old man Van Loan."

"Did he approve the marriage?" put in the Chemist.

"No, he did not. But after it had taken place he seemed inclined to make the best of it. Robert Blake is not an unlikable chap—you will all meet him shortly. His father-in-law gave them the bungalow, and a small car—a flivver, as the type is sometimes called. James Blake continued living in a boarding house nearby; and both brothers still hold their positions with the Tonola Company.

"This brings us to the tragedy of a week ago. The young

wife was indisposed. Her husband was sleeping in the room adjoining their bedroom. They have a maid who does not sleep in the house. Robert, about three in the morning, telephoned his father-in-law. He had been awakened by what sounded like a scuffle in the bedroom—heard his wife fall. He found her lying on the floor—dead. Death was caused, as has since been determined, by a blow on the head by some blunt instrument. A fractured skull and a brain concussion, I believe.

"There was no weapon in the room. The windows, which are only a few feet above the ground, were open because of the heat. A corner of the mahogany bureau was found to bear blood stains, and there was a smear of blood on one of the window sills. That, I think, represents the entire evidence at the scene of the crime."

The Doctor paused. A heavy rain outside was driving against the window panes; for a moment it was the only sound that broke the stillness of the room.

"It seems to me," the Alienist remarked finally, "that most of the facts rest upon what the husband says."

"Quite so," the Doctor agreed. "Naturally that puts him under suspicion. On the other hand, there is no motive—"

"Her money," suggested the Lawyer.

"I don't see that," the Chemist disagreed. "That might have been his motive for marrying her—not for killing her. As I understand it, the girl had no money in her own right. The financial attraction might have been what her father presumably would do for them—the house and car, for instance. With the girl's death all that ceases. No, I think that's an argument *for* the husband, rather than against him."

The other leaped to his feet, flinging his chair back with a crash.

"What's this older brother got to do with it?" the Banker demanded. "What's his name? I haven't read the confounded thing at all—I hate murders."

The Doctor smiled. "The only material thing that connects James Blake with the affair is that a railroad spike—bloodstained, and too smeared with dirt to bear fingerprints—was found under a tree behind the boarding house where he lives, and almost immediately below the window of his room."

"Where *was* James Blake during that night?" asked the Astronomer.

"He says he was at home in bed. He might have been. Also he could easily have gone out for a few hours—he has a latch-key."

"I've thought right along that he did it," the Inventor declared.

The Lawyer put in: "I take the opposite view. Knowing nothing much of the case, from what I've read I incline toward the husband."

The Doctor raised his hand. "Don't let us waste time with personal opinions, gentlemen. There's no object in going into all the clues and motives. That is a matter for professional sleuths. The police have questioned both these young men—have threatened them in every way possible. The result is nil.

"Neither will say anything beyond the story as I have given it to you. Police methods have failed, at least so far. This murder may have been committed by either of these two brothers, or by a third party. All the evidence is police work. We cannot attempt it."

"What can we attempt?" the Banker demanded.

The Doctor's voice took on an added earnestness. "I propose, gentlemen, merely to assume that one of these two brothers is guilty. I will discard all evidence, either for or against them. Either they are guilty or they are not. And they *know*, without regard to what we may *think*."

"You're just going to ask them nicely to tell us the real truth, I suppose?" the Banker commented sarcastically.

The Doctor did not smile. "I am going to do something the police have never done—could not do—but we here in the Scientific Club can do it very easily. To use against them as my only weapon the power of—"

A knock on the door interrupted him; an attendant announced:

"Mr. Robert Blake is here to see Dr. Adams."

The Doctor said hastily: "Enough, gentlemen—here he is. Jack, are we ready?"

The Very Young Man nodded soberly; his heightened color betrayed his suppressed excitement. "Yes, sir. Everything—all ready."

The Doctor had no more than time to say swiftly: "Just follow my lead, gentlemen. Do what I tell you—and say nothing," and the men had settled themselves about the room with the newspapers gathered up and put away, when their visitor stood in the doorway.

He was a dark-haired young man, rather tall and powerfully built, a smooth-shaven, somewhat handsome face in a bold, rugged way, the type of face that many women find immediately attractive. He stared in surprise at the number of men in the room, all of whom were eying him curiously.

The Doctor rose immediately to greet him. "Come in, Mr. Blake. Gentlemen, this is Robert Blake, husband of the unfortunate young woman who met her death last week. I have asked him here because I think it just possible that we may be able to help him solve the mystery of his wife's death. He tells me that is what he wishes, and I know, if there *is* anything we can do— Sit down, Mr. Blake. I need not introduce these gentlemen separately. Like myself, they are all members of the Scientific Club here."

Robert Blake sat down a little awkwardly. "I don't see there is anything you gentlemen can do—I mean it's awfully good of you—I'll tell you anything I can, of course."

His accent was noticeably British, his voice deep-toned and pleasing.

"We do not want to distress you unnecessarily, Mr. Blake," the Doctor said gently. "But we'd like to have you tell us in your own words—just what occurred the night of the tragedy."

"I will—yes, of course," assented the visitor. His glance roved over the intent faces before him.

"I'm afraid I'm going to disappoint you," he added

frankly. "I fancy you've read everything I know about it. But I *do* wish you could help me find out who—who killed poor Edith." His eyes suddenly flashed; his big strong fingers worked convulsively. "If I could get my hands on whoever did that to Edith, I'd—"

"I like him," the Very Young Man whispered impulsively to the Astronomer beside him.

The Doctor said kindly: "Tell us just what you know occurred—never mind if you think we've heard it before."

Robert Blake spoke for perhaps five minutes—a straightforward, earnest recital. To what the Doctor had already given as an outline of the case he added practically nothing.

"What's your brother got to do with it?" the Banker asked abruptly.

The youthful visitor flushed; then went pale. "Why—er, nothing, sir, that I know of."

"You don't think he had anything to do with it?" the Chemist put in. He exchanged a glance with the Doctor whose expression seemed warning him to stop.

The Doctor interposed quickly: "He has already answered that for the police. He does not want to suspect his own brother."

Before Robert could answer, there came another knock on the door.

"Dr. Adams—Mr. James Blake to see you."

The door closed. The Doctor added quickly: "Gentlemen, there is only one question I have wanted to ask this young man. I'll ask it now." He stood before Robert, who at the announcement of his brother's name had uttered a single, startled cry.

"Robert Blake, did *you* murder your wife?"

Robert's gaze swung up to his questioner's face. "No, sir, I did not," he answered steadily.

The Doctor relaxed. The door opened and James Blake was ushered into the room. His resemblance to his brother was considerable, but James was the smaller of the two, not so much in height as in slenderness of frame. His face was without Robert's rugged strength, a quiet, almost studious face, with solemn dark eyes. He stood in the doorway a moment, in his turn surprised by the number of men in the room.

Then after an instant he noticed his brother. Hate leaped into his eyes—unmistakable hate; and every man in the room saw it. He gave a sudden, half-suppressed exclamation but recovered himself quickly. Robert met his gaze; their glances crossed, then both looked away.

"Come in, Mr. Blake," the Doctor greeted.

Introductions were made. The newcomer smiled, and took the chair the Doctor offered. "I came at Dr. Adams's request," he said. "It is very good of you gentlemen—"

He spoke quietly, his precise manner making him seem older than he really was.

The Doctor interrupted him. "That is our object—to help you, Mr. Blake—" He turned to the club members. "My connection with this affair is quite simple, gentlemen. I am an old friend of Mr. Van Loan's—"

Both brothers seemed to start as he said it, but his friendly smile reassured them.

"An old friend—and I knew poor Edith Blake very well. Hence, I have a personal interest in these two young gentlemen who now, by marriage, are connected with the family. They are both suspected of this murder—unjustly, I have no doubt—"

The Doctor's keen gaze alternated between the two young men, "Each of you is unfortunately under suspicion—although as yet the police do not seem to feel that they have enough evidence to take drastic action."

"We—" James Blake began; but the Doctor's gesture silenced him.

"One moment, please. It is at Mr. Van Loan's suggestion that I have asked you both to come here. Mr. Van Loan feels that this was a chance murder by some outside marauder. He wants you two young men cleared if possible—wants the case hushed up. His daughter is dead—no power on this earth can bring her back. And so, most of all, he wishes to avoid any public sensationalism. An arrest—"

Again both brothers started involuntarily.

"An arrest, a trial—all that sort of thing which would make the Van Loan family a public spectacle—that is what he wishes to avoid. Do you young men understand me?"

They both nodded solemnly.

"Quite so," said the Doctor. "You will understand, then, that we of the Scientific Club here are occasionally involved in private affairs of this character. What goes on within these walls is seldom made public, and yet our testimony, given privately to the police, is not without its weight. Just a moment more, then you can question me."

His gaze included all the men in the room. "Gentlemen, I have asked you here this evening to be witnesses as well as spectators. I believe that we can clear these two brothers of all suspicion of the murder of Edith Blake. Clear them, you understand, once and for all. Present our evidence to the police, and then—" He shrugged.

"Well, if the professional sleuths can locate some third party as the murderer, well and good. If not—Mr. Van Loan will be quite pleased to let the case drop."

A relief seemed to have come to the brothers, but the Doctor's next words dispelled it.

"To that end, gentlemen, I am planning to make—here and now—an experiment—a test, if you will—which I believe will clear these two young men completely."

"A test!" They both murmured it with evident alarm.

"Yes. Call it that." A note of dominance came to the Doctor's tone. "A test, to clear you. As I say, scientific evidence which we have sometimes been able to gather here in the club carries considerable weight with the authorities. When properly attested by a group of our members, it—"

He broke off, and raised his hand deprecatingly. "Of course, if either of you brothers care to refuse, if the thought of making yourself the subject of a scientific experiment is repugnant, we have no wish and no power to force you. We can only give the police our report that you refused. An unfortunate implication, of course—"

James's eyes came up from the floor. "I—I'm quite ready to do anything you advise," he declared. And his younger brother echoed it.

"Frightened!" murmured the Astronomer. "Look at them—both frightened."

"Anyone would be," the Chemist whispered back. "Innocent or guilty. But one of them did it. Dr. Adams feels convinced of that."

The Doctor's quiet voice went on: "Thank you. I knew you would say that. You need not be perturbed. To the layman, the very words 'scientific experiment' sound awe-inspiring. That is only natural. But let me assure you, you will not be hurt, you will not even have to undergo anything unpleasant."

His assurances seemed to bring no relief to the brothers; but each endeavored to smile. By their demeanor either of them could readily have been assumed innocent or guilty. They were obviously trying to repress their perturbation— or fear; indeed, of all the men in the room, the Very Young Man, waiting to do his part in aiding the Doctor, was visibly the most excited.

"What is your—your experiment, Dr. Adams?" Robert Blake asked, a trifle unsteadily. He swept a sidelong glance at James; but the older brother was staring stolidly before him.

The Doctor answered: "I'm coming to that in a moment. Let me proceed in my own way if you don't mind." Again he addressed the room in general.

"Gentlemen, we have here a very simple problem. To summarize it for you: This Robert Blake, who may have murdered his young bride…. Sit down, young man! You must realize I am talking theoretically. I said you *may* have murdered Edith Blake. That is true, isn't it?"

"Why, yes, I—I suppose theoretically it is. Only—"

"You know you did not," the Doctor finished. "Quite so. You know it—but we don't. Again, gentlemen, as I was saying, we have here this young husband who may have murdered his wife. For any one of a thousand motives which are unknown to us.

"And on the other hand, we have this older brother James. A blood-stained railroad spike was found under his window. Was that spike the weapon with which the murder was committed? Possibly."

The Doctor's voice grew very earnest. "Gentlemen, all that sort of evidence does not concern us. The motives, facts, and details underlying a murder usually have tremendous ramifications. We are not trained to analyze such details. Personally, I want no evidence.

"I assume that at the moment of the tragedy, Robert Blake was in the room adjoining his wife's bedroom—and that James Blake was at home in his boarding house. I do not propose to proceed with theories, with questioning of these two witnesses, with deductions of my own. I am going to discard all the usual methods of solving a criminal mystery. I know very little of this affair—what little I do know, I will ignore.

"I want to free these brothers from the suspicion hanging over them—which might otherwise always hang over them. And I want only to ask Mr. James Blake one question—the same question I have already asked his brother."

The Doctor's glance, darting from one face to another among his hearers, came suddenly to rest on James Blake. "Did *you* murder Edith Blake?"

James's gaze held steady. "No, sir, I did not."

The Doctor relaxed, seemingly relieved. "Quite so. Both you and Robert we then presume and believe to be innocent. I now propose to prove it to the satisfaction of the police. That would be very agreeable to you, would it not?" His smile was friendly, almost cordial.

"Quite so. Naturally that is what you wish. And for Mr.

Van Loan's sake—because he is my friend—that is what I hope we will accomplish. Jack, will you go in and get the apparatus ready? I'll call you when I want you."

The Very Young Man rose hastily and went into an adjoining room, closing the door after him.

The Doctor resumed quietly: "I think only one or two of you gentlemen have ever seen this demonstration, or even know that we have perfected the apparatus with which to make it. Professor Watson has done it, and though he is not here this evening. I want to state I have been merely his very inefficient assistant in the research work. It has not been made public yet, for it is still barely past the experimental stage. I must ask you all—and you, James and Robert Blake—to repeat nothing of what you learn here this evening."

The two brothers nodded. They seemed still apprehensive—anxious to hear what they were being asked to do. It was Robert who voiced the anxiety.

The Doctor smiled: "If you will be patient just a moment longer. Most of you gentlemen will need no explanation of the scientific principles involved in Professor Watson's revolutionary apparatus, but to these young men I will explain briefly.

He began addressing the brothers directly. "We are to deal with vibrations. To be almost absurdly simple, let me tell you that light is vibration. Visible vibration, as we commonly know it. And sound is audible vibration. You understand me?"

"Yes," they murmured.

"Quite so. Let me go further. There are light vibrations which are invisible to the human eye. They lie—to be a little technical—below the red of the spectrum—very slow vibrations which we call the infra-red. And beyond the violet lie the ultra-violet, which are too rapid to be visible.

"That is all clear, no doubt. Thus also, there are sounds we cannot hear, just as there is light we cannot see. The range of our human senses is very limited. Radio waves we might call inaudible sound. And there exist other vibrations as well—the X-ray, for instance—many vibrations which we have discovered—and doubtless many more still unknown to us.

"I come now to the direct matter in hand." The Doctor was watching the two brothers narrowly. "There is a vibration the existence of which for many years has been suspected. It could be—if we knew how to harness it, so to speak—as useful and as common as light or sound. Sir William Crookes, I think, was first to mention its existence." The Doctor paused slightly. "It is the vibration of *thought*, gentlemen."

There was a stir in the room, Robert Blake murmured something, but James still sat stolid.

"The vibration of thought," the Doctor repeated. He went on, somewhat faster but still quietly: "That needs some explanation. The fact that thought, as well as heat, light and sound, is a vibration, has for some time been believed. I mean, gentlemen, that the human brain is continually sending out vibrations. A sending station of thought waves. But, since there is no receiving station, they go to waste.

"It is no new theory, and even before Professor Watson's time, there was considerable proof of its correctness. The Yogis of India have demonstrated it for centuries, if you

care to believe their proof. I have seen them shatter a fragile globe of glass, presumably by the thought waves they
could send against it.

"But that is not our science. Telepathy is. We, none of us
here, believe in spiritualism, perhaps, but we cannot deny
telepathy. There is your receiving station, gentlemen! Some
human brain capable of receiving the thought vibrations
which some other brain is sending out. It is no more mysterious than radio, and quite comparable.

"I must be briefer. We are not concerned with telepathy—I mention it merely as an example. In a word, Professor Watson—with some slight assistance from me—has
perfected an instrument for the receiving of thought vibrations. Ah, now you get my drift, Robert and James Blake!
Do not be perturbed. It will not hurt you—not even be
unpleasant. And you are not forced to do it. Either of you
may withdraw now if you wish."

The Doctor's tone took on a sudden menace, but he was
still smiling. "Now is your time to withdraw. Either of you
who fears this demonstration. But I warn you—by police
reasoning it will be equal to a confession of guilt."

The Blakes hesitated; looked at each other—defiantly,
it seemed.

"I—I don't want to withdraw," stammered James.

"No," echoed Robert.

"Very good," smiled the Doctor. "Naturally not, since
you would lose an opportunity of proving your innocence.
Rogers, open that door and call Jack Bruce, will you?"

The Chemist opened the door to the adjoining room.
From where the men sat nothing was visible in there save

a big screen behind which the Very Young Man was working. "Oh, Jack—Dr. Adams is ready, if you are."

"I'm ready." The Very Young Man emerged from behind
the screen and entered the main room. He was carrying
a black-painted board some three feet square, on which
was assembled an apparatus of coils and wires. A small
black metal box with tuning dials; two very small horns,
each no more than three inches in diameter, mounted side
by side so that they were almost touching; wires running
from them to the metal box; and from the box, other wires
connecting with an upright frame some two feet high,
upon which fully a hundred tiny wires were strung like a
harp.

A strange-looking apparatus dead-black, mysterious,
and businesslike. As the Very Young Man carried it in,
the scientific men regarded it with interest, several whispering to their neighbors. The brothers gazed with awe,
perturbation, and what possibly was fear. Was it a natural
fear, which any innocent man would feel upon the brink
of lending himself as the subject of a mysterious scientific
experiment? Or fear born of the knowledge of guilt? No
one in the room could have told, though every eye was
watching them keenly. Did either of them wish to withdraw? Very possibly. But it was obvious that neither dared
to show it.

"Place it here, Jack." The Doctor shoved a table against
the wall close to the door of the adjoining room; and on
the table the Very Young Man laid the apparatus.

"The lights, Jack. And will you lock those other doors?
We must have no interruption now. And you gentlemen—

will you move aside, please? We want these two young men in the center."

It took only a moment to arrange the room. The Very Young Man locked its outer doors, removing the keys and slipping them in his pocket; the club members shifted aside, so that in the center a space was cleared where the Doctor placed two small chairs side by side. The chairs faced the apparatus on the table over a distance of some ten feet.

"Quite so. Now—will you young men please seat yourselves here?"

They hesitated. Both were very solemn, trembling but holding themselves firm. Reluctant, and yet obviously they had gone too far to back out now.

The Doctor added quickly: "This will not hurt you. I promise you that. My only hope is that it will work, and thus prove your innocence." His voice, striving to be convincing, grew apologetic. "As I told Mr. Van Loan, this apparatus is as yet in a very experimental stage—it may conceivably prove a total failure in this instance—but for your sakes, I hope not."

His words seemed at last to bring a measure of relief to the brothers. James stood up. "I'm ready, Dr. Adams."

They took the chairs, sitting stiff and tense, eying the two little horns which, side by side, were pointed directly at them.

The Doctor smiled. "Very good. Turn off those other lights, Jack."

As the Very Young Man obeyed, shadows sprang up about the room. Its corners and walls were in gloom. All the lights were out except one fixture which hung from the ceiling in the center; its dome-shaped shade threw a yellow circle down upon the brothers. But the rest of the room was in semi-darkness. And suddenly very silent; only the shifting feet of the watching scientists, and the sound of the Very Young Man fumbling with the apparatus on the table.

The Doctor was standing in the shadows to one side. "One last word of explanation, gentlemen. Thought vibrations, like the vibrations of radio, are normally inaudible, of course. But they can—like radio—be transformed into vibrations which our ears can hear. It is this function and none other, which Professor Watson's apparatus is designed to perform. Merely the transforming—the magnifying, let me say, of these extremely minute vibrations of thought— bringing them up within the range of our human ears, so that we may hear them."

The Doctor's watchful eyes saw the brothers glance side- wise at each other; but neither spoke, nor seemed daring to move. And it became apparent now that there was no guilty collusion between them. Nothing but animosity. If one were guilty—the other doubtless was innocent.

"Are you ready, Jack?"

"Yes, sir. All ready."

A tiny light on the table was now glowing, making visi- ble the two little horns and the upright frame of wires.

"Good. Now you, James and Robert Blake, must sit quiet and calm. Not so tense. There, that's better—I want you to relax. Let your mind rove back over the night Edith Blake was murdered. Tell yourself that you have nothing to fear—that this experiment, if it is successful, will surely prove your innocence of the murder. You *know*—each of you—whether you are innocent or not. We want your thoughts! We want to hear them from those little horns. Your thoughts of what each of you was doing at the time Edith Blake was murdered!"

The room fell oppressively silent. Breathless. A moment, and then the wires in the upright frame seemed beginning to vibrate. A little at first, then more and more until a faint hum was coming from them. Another moment; and from the twin horns—faint whispers! Incoherent. Then louder. Whispers growing audible, resolving into voices—tiny aerial voices.

One horn whispering: *"I didn't do it! I'm innocent! I didn't do it!"*

The other: *"They'll never get me! I did it, but they'll never get me!"*

Mingled, blended whispers, yet now plainly audible, repeating over and over:

"I'm innocent! I'm innocent!"

"They'll never get me! They'll never get me!"

For an instant, in the yellow circle of light, the brothers sat tense. Then one gave a low exclamation of relief; the other—Robert Blake, the young husband—leaped to his feet, flinging his chair from him with a crash.

"Turn that damn thing off! Turn it off, I say! I did it! You know that now—that damn thing knows it! You've got me. Turn it off, I say!"

With the horns still whispering, his almost incoherent confession came. He had married this Edith Blake—two years older than himself—a cultured, refined, but not a pretty girl—married her for her money—won her from his older brother, who probably really loved her. Married her for the money he hoped to get out of the Van Loan family—and then found that no money was coming to him. None, except a modest little bungalow and a cheap automobile.

A quarrel, because she would not wheedle money from her mother, at her husband's insistence, and he had tried to make her take some of her mother's jewels so that he might pawn or sell them, and she had threatened to tell her father. A quarrel—his violent temper—anger uncontrollable, unreasoning—in which he had flung her against the mahogany bureau—striking her head—killing her. Terrified, he had tried to cover his crime. Smeared blood on the window sill, to make it look as though someone had escaped that way.

Found an old railroad spike—smeared it with blood—dropped it under his brother's window, trying to think quickly what he ought to do before he telephoned his father-in-law. His brother had been his unsuccessful rival—suspicion would fall on him very easily.

It was a commonplace crime. Almost motiveless, as are nine out of ten with which the police have to deal. And for that very reason almost unsolvable by ordinary methods.

Robert Blake poured it all out before those twenty witnesses. The tiny horns had ceased their whisperings. From the shadows came the Doctor's voice:

"Jack! Oh, Jack!"

The door to the adjoining room opened. It was dark in there. The Very Young Man had gone in there some time before, closing the door quietly after him. But none had noticed his departure.

"Oh, Jack, light these lights, will you?"

The lights sprang on. The men saw Robert Blake standing trembling, and James Blake sitting tense, eying his guilty brother with a stolid hate.

"Jack, will you phone for the police? Tell them we have a confession from one of the Blake brothers of Maple Grove—and we're holding him here. The other brother we have exonerated. And phone out to Mr. Van Loan—tell him we have solved it."

The Doctor faced the room. "Gentlemen, forgive me if I have in any way exaggerated the powers of our wires and coils and horns. We cannot make the vibrations of thought audible as yet, gentlemen—as you well know, of course. But in this case we have done just as well. I know you will not feel defrauded when I tell you that Jack Bruce in the next room spoke those whispers into a telephone. In the darkness, a while ago, Jack Bruce plugged a telephone wire from that apparatus into a socket near the floor over there. From the next room it was he who operated a very simple electric connection which made that frame of wires vibrate so impressively; and he who by telephone gave those whispers we heard from the horns. One whisper proclaimed innocence—the other, guilt. But which was which? None of us could have told. None of us knew. But James and Robert Blake knew. And so curious is the human mind that each of them instinctively took to himself the whisper which applied.

"The point is, gentlemen," and a note of exultation rang in his voice, "the point is, gentlemen, that our little apparatus *did* make thoughts audible. James and Robert Blake have demonstrated that fact incontrovertibly in these last fifteen minutes."

The Doctor Paused slightly. "I think that's all, gentlemen. Our experiment is over."

THE MURDER IN THE POOL

"HE WAS MURDERED only last evening," said the Doctor. "Here in our own pool at the club, during the game of water polo."

Some ten members of the Scientific Club were grouped before the Doctor in the small private clubroom. To one side sat a young man in his early twenties, a stalwart, athletic-looking youth, strong-featured, pink and white face, blue eyes and closely clipped wavy brown hair, a typical specimen of young American manhood. He sat staring at the floor, his attitude constrained and solemn.

The Doctor's glance turned to him momentarily—an anxious, perturbed glance.

"Most of you gentlemen were there," the Doctor went on. "You saw the murder committed, as I did myself."

"I wasn't there," the Alienist spoke up.

"No, Dr. Gregg. For you and two or three of the others I'll describe the affair briefly. I'm sorry I couldn't consult some of you in advance about this. But I've been rushed—anxious—worried—you know how it is—"

The Doctor stopped as he began to flounder. To those who knew him—who had heard him conduct in his calm, professional, almost pedantic manner many strange affairs in this same club—this was a very different Dr. Adams who now sat before them.

His thin face, with its rimless glasses and neatly pointed Vandyke, was flushed and harassed. He spoke hurriedly, awkwardly. It was not an overly warm night, but the beads of perspiration stood on his forehead until he mopped them away.

"I'll describe it to you very briefly, gentlemen. You all know my son, Roy, of course. Roy, will you—will you stand up, please?"

The Doctor's voice was affectionate, but firmly commanding. The youth stood up obediently. He flushed more deeply under the glances directed at him, but his lean jaw was set firm and his gaze held level.

"My son, gentlemen. Does he—look like a murderer?"

The Chemist murmured, "Frank, don't be absurd."

The Doctor caught the words and swung about. "Not absurd, Rogers. He—my son is under arrest at this present moment. You know that perfectly well—you all know it—know that he's only at liberty because I furnished bail." His gaze included all the men. He smiled, a grim smile with pathos struggling under it, but his voice held clear and strong.

"In this room, gentlemen, I've faced many people suspected of murder—faced them calmly—judged them by scientific theory—accused them by theory, practical psychology—what you will. And in many cases I have forced from them the truth. My son at this very moment stands before us like those others—suspected of murder. Am I going to spare him because I'm his father? He—"

The Doctor faltered just a little, in spite of his protestations. "He—will have to take his chance—like those others. Sit down, Roy. I—"

The Very Young Man, who was sitting tense and grim beside Roy Adams, spoke up vehemently:

"He didn't do it, Dr. Adams. You know that. It's damn nonsense. I was right there in the game, and I'm positive about it all. Why, Roy didn't know this Robert Mack any better than I did. What would he murder him for?"

As Roy sat down, the Very Young Man gripped his arm, murmuring to him indignantly.

The Doctor said soberly: "Quite right, Jack. I suppose there is no one in the room here—least of all myself—who could imagine Roy being guilty. But the police may imagine it—in fact they arrested him with those two others—"

"They're crazy!" the Very Young Man declared angrily. "But, of course, they have to arrest somebody."

The Doctor smiled faintly. "That's the way we instinctively feel about it, of course. But we have only Roy's word that he's innocent. That isn't very much evidence, Jack."

"I was right in the game, I tell you."

"Yes," agreed the Doctor. "And you saw—nothing. You've told everything you could to the police. It isn't evidence, because you—like everyone else—saw nothing and—legally speaking—know nothing about it at all."

"That's exactly the way *I* stand," interjected the Banker testily. "I know nothing about it at all—and it doesn't seem likely that I'll find out anything about it, listening to *you.*"

The Doctor made an effort to smile. "I'm sorry, George. If I'm incoherent, you'll understand it's—"

"Because they've arrested your son, as I gather," the Banker finished. "It's nonsense, getting excited over a thing like that. Arrest Roy? Have 'em in here—these crazy policemen—I'll tell 'em a thing or two. Who got murdered?

"My chance will come—I must have that knife!"

How did it happen? I've asked twenty people and they're all too incoherent to tell me."

The Doctor said: "You're consoling, George. Of course it's all nonsense, as you say. But it's very real, just the same. They're working on it—these 'crazy policemen,' you call them. Suppose it came to trial—suppose circumstances—circumstantial evidence against Roy—it *has* convicted upon occasion. Or, even if not, even if nothing came of it. His mother, you know—she's quite prostrated, gentlemen—"

"You're excited," said the Banker, though not unkindly. "And Frank, listen, if you've got any experiment or anything to work here tonight, take my advice and get a grip on yourself. If you don't, you'll fail."

Nothing else that he could have said would have been more efficacious.

"You're perfectly right, George." The Doctor was visibly forcing himself to calmness. His hands, which had been gripping tensely the sides of his chair, relaxed. "Gentlemen, we'll forget Roy, forget who he is, I mean as my son. A case of murder, gentlemen, with three suspects and practically no evidence—"

"You're going to give us the details?" the Banker interrupted gently.

"Yes. Last evening there was a game of water-polo played in the club pool downstairs. Our Scientific Club team— the sons of our members—played against the Wisconsin Dolphins, a team from Pollin University."

"We played them last year," the Very Young Man put in. "The N.Y.U. fixes it up—that's all we know about it. This Robert Mack—Roy and I never heard of him, except we met him last year. Why would Roy—"

"Quite true," the Doctor interrupted. "At all events, the Dolphins arrived in New York yesterday—a match arranged, as Jack says, by the N.Y.U. During the game, gentlemen—most of you saw it—this Robert Mack of the Dolphins had the ball. He was not far from our basket. My son—" The Doctor compressed his lips. "This young Adams here, according to the consensus of eye-witness testimony, was nearest to Mack. He flung his arms about Mack's neck before the ball could be thrown. The two went down together. Mack later released the ball. It bobbed to the surface. Some other Dolphin player—I don't know who—seized it—tossed it in—"

"Grant," supplied the Very Young Man. "I was on the surface, I saw it, but I couldn't get there."

The Doctor nodded. "This young fellow Adams came up, but Mack didn't come up. They brought him up—dead, with a small thin-bladed dagger buried to the hilt in his back."

The Doctor was breathing a little heavily. "That's all, gentlemen."

"What do you mean, that's all?" growled the Banker. "See here, Roy, what about it?"

2

YOUNG ADAMS SPOKE quietly but with level tones that carried throughout the silent room.

"That's about all I know, too, sir. I pulled Mack under, blocking his throw. There seemed to be no one near us at the moment. Mack fought me to get loose, but I clung, and we went down nearly to the bottom of the tank, I think. I couldn't see much—my face was against Mack's chest; I was gripping him low.

"I was conscious other players were diving for us, trying to get the ball as he released it. Somebody was behind Mack. I couldn't tell who. Then—well, then Mack let go of the ball. I cast him off, and went up to the surface. Then, when—Mack didn't come up we found he was—was murdered."

There was a brief silence, then the Doctor said:

"No details, you see, gentlemen? There is the story of—of one of the suspects. There are two others—both Dolphin players—both of whom disappeared under the surface toward Mack. And both of whom, curiously enough, reappeared some distance away. They are, by name, George Hotchkiss and Arthur Jones. Both are in custody. There has been no time for bail to be supplied—the relations of them both live in the far West. Marberry will bring them here this evening—any moment."

"What are their stories?" the Lawyer demanded.

"They each tell about the same thing. They saw Mack and his—his adversary go down. Dived for them, hoping to secure the ball when it was released."

"You see," interrupted the Very Young Man, "if you can get the ball on its way up—"

The Doctor raised his hand. "That's immaterial, Jack. They both dove, almost to the bottom of the pool. They went too low. At all events, as they tell it, before they reached Mack they saw the ball ascending. They returned to the surface."

The Chemist said: "Neither of them saw anything of the murder?"

"No, they say not. Nor did anyone else, players or spectators."

"But why—" began the Lawyer, but the Alienist had spoken first.

"Can't the spectators see into the water?"

The Doctor shook his head. "If we had a balcony they could, to some extent. But from near the surface, the light is reflected. This Mack was at one end, but he was near the middle line of the pool. And the water was lashed and turbulent. Quite impossible to see down into it."

"I was going to say," the Lawyer cut in, "these other two suspected players—you say they both reappeared some distance away? Was that normal? Or perhaps, did one or both swim away to avoid suspicion?"

"I don't know," the Doctor answered. "Detective Marberry raised the point. Evidently it was fairly normal."

"It was," interrupted the Very Young Man. "You see,

when Grant got the ball—that is, *if* they saw that he had it—then their play was to—"

"We don't want to learn how to play the game," interrupted the Banker. "You're after something tonight, Frank? What is it?"

The Doctor hesitated for a moment as though phrasing what he had to say. He began slowly: "Yes, I am, George, and I'm trying to handle this, as I've handled other cases—you understand me—without personal feeling." He stopped short, began again:

"You see, gentlemen, this is one of those cases which by its very simplicity, its lack of detail, may easily be extremely baffling. Simple murders are, as a rule, the most difficult to solve."

"May I interrupt?" the Lawyer put in. At the Doctor's nod the Lawyer said: "I was thinking of the weapon. No fingerprints on it, probably. But it seems to me odd that one of these players—whichever one may be guilty—could have successfully concealed a dagger. His scanty swimming suit—"

"I should have mentioned it," said the Doctor. "The police—Marberry—went into it thoroughly. I have the weapon here; it was loaned me unofficially because—" His voice trailed off.

"Frank," interjected the Banker sharply.

The Doctor smiled. "I'm not my usual methodical self, am I? But I will be in a moment, when the others get here. I'm worried not so much over Roy as his mother, gentlemen. A sort of hysteria has fallen upon her. The shock, I suppose. I can't seem to get her out of it." He pulled himself up short.

"Gentlemen, to be candid, I'm trying something tonight rather hastily planned. For my wife's sake I don't want to wait. I must settle it now; exonerate Roy—if only I can—"

"What about the dagger?" demanded the Banker.

"Oh, yes, of course." The Doctor produced it from a table drawer, a slender affair with a blade no more than six or eight inches long. It was in a sheath.

The men crowded around to examine it. The Doctor said: "I don't know the material of this sheath—leather, I imagine—but without the dagger, it sinks. It was found lying on the bottom of the pool, just about under where Mack must have been when he was stabbed."

The Doctor held up the sheath. It was green-white in color, and mottled.

"Selected, gentlemen, evidently because it would be barely visible in water. Marberry showed us that at once. His theory is that the murderer smuggled it into the pool previously, during the late afternoon practice perhaps. Hid it under the ladder, possibly, or perhaps merely laid it on the bottom in a corner. It probably would never be noticed. Then, during the game, at an opportune moment, he secured it—struck the blow as he dropped the sheath—"

"I see," agreed the Lawyer.

"Such is Marberry's assumption," the Doctor went on. "As I was saying, gentlemen, I want very much to clear this thing up at once. There is, as yet, practically no evidence. No possible motive is known. I wired to Pollin University for information concerning these other two suspects: this George Hotchkiss and this Arthur Jones. And, of course, the other Dolphin players told me and the police a good deal.

"So far as the police could see, there was nothing to choose between them and this—them and Roy. Except that they obviously, being schoolmates of Mack, must have had greater opportunity for a motive. Roy had none that I know of.

"But Roy was closest to Mack—was actually grappling with him, as the authorities very curtly told me. They also say that Roy is the only one positively proven to have been within striking distance of Mack. Gripping him face to face, he could easily have stabbed him in the back.

"So you see—I was saying, the motive isn't necessary, gentlemen. This morning an idea came to me, an idea which scientifically you would all appreciate. I discussed it with Marberry; we examined the body. My theory, gentlemen, would clearly indicate—from our scientific point of view—the identity of the murderer. I said nothing of it, except to Marberry, for in this instance our science would not constitute legal proof. A corroborating circumstance— yes. But of itself it would fail to convict."

The Doctor's voice rose to vehement power. "You see what I mean, gentlemen? If this scientific circumstance, let me say, were divulged in the usual way, the young man would stand firm against it. And the case might never be solved. Roy, all his life, would have the stigma against him. And his mother—

"I mean, gentlemen, I'm forced to take the thing into my own hands at once. I wired to the faculty of Pollin University. They answered. I got their wire this afternoon. It gave me a clear basis for a thing which—"

3

"**DETECTIVE MARBERRY IS** here, Dr. Adams."

The Doctor rose from his chair. His hand was shaking as he pulled open the table drawer and hastily replaced the small dagger in its sheath.

"Bring them up. There are two young men with him?"

"Yes, sir." The attendant withdrew, returning in a moment with Detective Marberry, a uniformed officer, and the two prisoners. Marberry greeted the club members quietly and seated himself. The policeman took a position near the door.

The Doctor fronted the two young men. "You will sit down, please. You need not concern yourselves with these gentlemen. It is I who sent for you."

Sullenly, yet with a youthful defiant bravado, they seated themselves, gazing stolidly at the men who all were eying them attentively. Both were young men in their early twenties. Arthur Jones was tall, slim, yet muscular; broad-shouldered, narrow of hip. A perfect type of athlete. Graceful of movement, a handsome face, dark eyes, a dark skin bronzed by the sun almost to a golden sheen, and smooth, black hair.

Once, when momentarily he smiled, his face lighted up with the spark of an engaging personality—a smile of perfect white teeth parting his rather full red lips. An interesting-looking young man—and, to the practiced eye, a born swimmer.

His companion, George Hotchkiss, was of a wholly different type. He came into the room on crutches, which as he sat down he laid on the floor beside him. Standing with his crutches, Hotchkiss was well below medium height. His legs were shriveled. One barely touched the ground, the other dangled, twisted and deformed and no larger than the leg of a child.

A case of infantile paralysis. And as sometimes happens, the man's strength had gone into his torso. From the waist up Hotchkiss was of massive, rugged strength. A build which, had his legs been in proportion, would have brought him well above two hundred pounds.

Yet there seemed on him not an ounce of fat, or even of superfluous flesh. His face, too, was cast in the same rugged mold. Square jawed, solid, with features rough-hewn, and skin burned by the sun to a deep red-brown.

Gazing at him, the man beside the Astronomer whispered:

"A cripple, and yet an athlete?"

The Astronomer answered: "In the water he's a marvel. Not so fast, because of his legs; but his buoyancy, and the strength in those arms! He's a tireless swimmer—the best man on the team."

The Very Young Man leaned toward them. "Coxswain of the crew, also."

The Doctor was saying: "It is I whom you have to deal with, young men. Roy, will you sit beside them, please?"

It was a stern, tight-lipped command. The Doctor was

on his feet. Outwardly calm now; his face a trifle white, his eyes blazing.

Young Adams shifted his chair; the three young men sat very nearly in a row, with the Doctor standing before them.

"This will take only a moment, I'm sure. You three young men—one of you murdered Robert Mack!" His sudden step forward startled them all. His voice was low, but infinitely menacing in its level coldness.

"One of you committed murder, here in this very building, last evening. The police have questioned you—and you've stood up against them. But I'm not going to question you. What motive one of you may have had does not concern me. I brought you here for only one purpose. To find out which one of you is guilty. I don't know now—but I will in a moment. You may hide your guilt from the police, but not from me."

He leveled an accusing finger, swaying it in an arc to include each of them. "You are going to do as I say—do you understand? A scientific, medical experiment, which will tell us infallibly the guilty man. You need not look alarmed—the innocent have nothing to fear. Science makes no error. Nor can you refuse me.

"Marberry—all of us—will make you submit, by force if necessary. And to refuse will acknowledge guilt. You know that—you are all intelligent enough to realize it without being told."

His grim laugh rang out. Then he swung to the club members, and his voice quieted.

"A word of explanation, gentlemen. I am about to deal with a question of chemistry of the blood. I won't weary you with technicalities—I'll be brief. For years I have been studying the chemistry of the human blood. A complex but marvelous fluid, this life-stream of ours. You know, of course, how it nourishes, builds, and fights disease. You know, too, that within it lie the inherited diseases, traits, the very personality of our ancestors. Latent forces—yet occasionally they come out."

Did his words bring sudden fear to the faces of two of the three young men? It seemed so. He went on, still appearing to ignore them:

"None of this is exactly pertinent either. We have to deal here with an obscure organism of the blood known as the *hormone*. But little is known of it as yet. A chemical substance, which travels through the bloodstream like a messenger from one group of tissue cells to excite another group of cells to activity. A poor definition—but it must serve.

"These *hormones*—these little messengers—are supposed to play an important though mysterious part in diseases attacking the body. But, gentlemen, they do more than that. Each of us has in his blood red corpuscles and white corpuscles—the leucocytes. In general structure the blood of every one of us is similar.

"Yet—it carries also our personality, gentlemen—our inheritance—everything which makes us what we are. Call it personality. Different for each one of us, wholly individual. It—this personality—doesn't lie in the corpuscles, but in the *hormones*. If one of us commits murder, the cause—the capacity for the crime, let me say—lies there.

"Do I make myself clear? To be more specific, I have found a way to examine these tiny organisms—to gauge their capacity for crime—or, if the crime has been very recently committed, to observe its mark left upon them. Not visually—that is absurd. To observe it by its effect upon my own mentality.

"You all know of blood transfusion, of course—the surgical introduction of one person's blood into the veins of another. Does that transfused blood carry with it any of the characteristics of the person from whom it was taken? The medical profession says not. Such ideas are sentimental, nothing more.

"But, gentlemen, with that transfused blood come *hormones*, which do in fact contain a personality. In the new veins they apparently do not act. I say apparently, because to the medical profession reports have come—in a few not very conclusive cases—where a transfusion seemed to alter the *character* of the person receiving the blood. In general, such reports are not credited by physicians. Yet, for myself, I know they are probably true—for the thing happened to me, in my youth."

4

HE PAUSED AN instant, eying the three young men, then turning back to the club members.

"Happened to me, gentlemen. At seventeen I was anemic. After an illness they resorted to a transfusion. My character did not alter exactly—certainly there was no permanent effect—but for some hours immediately after the transfusion I was obsessed with strange feelings. Not physical, but mental—strange desires surging within me. I need not describe them in detail—enough to say I seemed to feel a vague desire to commit violence."

The Doctor smiled. "Intangible feelings which wore off very soon, and which I promptly forgot—until a month later I learned that the man who had given me his blood had just been arrested for manslaughter.

"The thing seemed curious to me, and of recent years I have experimented with it—upon myself. A dangerous business—yet I have come through it safely. There are drugs, as you know, which temporarily weaken the moral fiber.

"This weakening, I found, made me still more susceptible to the dominance of—shall I say, alien personality? A drug addict—permanently weakened—may commit a murder if you urge him. But I mean the specific matter I am discussing.

"I found that while under the partial influence of certain drugs, alien blood brought into my brain quite distinct impressions from the brain through which it so recently had circulated. Impressions, I say? They are rather more like waking visions—not optical—my eyes see nothing abnormal. More like memories, gentlemen—mental pictures which are alien to me."

The Doctor was speaking more swiftly now, addressing the three young men directly.

"These mental pictures last no more than a moment—if the inoculation of blood be very small. I call it inoculation, not transfusion. That is a surgical matter—but to introduce into my veins a few drops of alien blood is simplicity itself. It brings swift, transitory alien impressions.

"The case in point here tonight is exceedingly favorable. This murder was committed no more than twenty-four hours ago. The blood disturbance inevitable during its commission has not had time to wear off. It will be strong and clear. It is now—this blood—circulating through the brain of this guilty young man—giving him memories.

"Ah! You understand me, don't you? Yes, I am under the influence of that demoralizing drug at this moment. I am susceptible, and—with your blood mingled with mine—I, too, will remember the details of your crime."

He ended in a note of ringing accusation. His son sat staring at him as though fascinated, but the other two were out of their chairs. Hotchkiss stood on one leg, supporting his swaying figure by gripping the table.

The Doctor swung away from them. "Dr. Gregg, my case is there in the corner. Get my hypodermic out, will you? A very simple matter—you'll do it for us, Dr. Gregg?"

He whirled back to the three young men. "A few drops of blood from each of you! A needle prick, nothing more. All three at once—the innocent blood will not affect me. You, Roy Adams—you understand?"

"Y-yes, sir."

"And you, Arthur Jones?"

"Why—why, yes. I—"

"And you, George Hotchkiss?"

The cripple raised his eyes. "I told you I didn't do it. I'm not—"

"You mean you refuse?"

"No. I—mean I'm not afraid, because I didn't do it."

"Of course—I understand. Ready, Dr. Gregg?"

It took only a moment. Amid dead silence throughout the room, the Alienist dabbed alcohol on the earlobe of each of the three suspects. A needle prick—a few drops of blood from each of them, mingled on a glass slide, drawn into the hypodermic, and inserted into a vein of the Doctor's wrist.

"Thank you, Dr. Gregg." The Doctor stood on his feet, his figure drooping and swaying. The men watched him silently; the three accused youths stood together—Roy Adams, perturbed and flushed, the other two white-faced and terror-stricken. Presently, with startling abruptness, the Doctor began to speak. Softly, vaguely at first, like one fumbling for words to picture a dream—or a memory.

" 'My chance will come suddenly. I must have that knife. I'll dive and get it—no one has seen it lying there.' That's what I told myself. I had the knife—swam with it. I can remember wondering if my swimming would look awkward. The whole thing was confused—my heart pounding—but my brain must have been clear."

The Doctor steadied himself against the table, across which George Hotchkiss was staring at him. The Doctor's voice began again.

"That's what it—yes, I can remember how my heart leaped when Mack got the ball. My chance! I saw young Adams had him around the neck. Dangerous for me—this thing! Queer I never realized the danger that I might be seen.

"Yet everyone was so interested in the game—players and spectators—everybody—of course no one but me was thinking of murder—yet it seemed as though everybody was. I wasn't under the water very long. Down there—I never knew the cripple was so near me—but he didn't see me—what luck—"

A cry rang through the room. Arthur Jones swept back his chair, his dark face bloodless—a green cast come to his swarthy skin, and his dark eyes blazing.

"You—I'm *not* thinking that! I can't remember anything like that, I tell you! God! The damn thing works, doesn't it?" He laughed wildly. "My blood giving me away—my curse Kanaka blood!"

With a bound, Detective Marberry was on him, gripping him by the shoulders. "You did it! You did, didn't you? You can't deny it now!"

"Yes, I did it. *He* knows I did it—how can I deny it? You know why? Ask him—he'll tell you. No, I'll tell you. That damned Robert Mack! I was engaged to a girl—I love her—I'd have married her—and that Mack told her my mother was a Kanaka.

"Tainted blood! He told her that—and told her father—and her father made her give me up. But Mack didn't get her, as he thought he would. I saw to that, and I'm glad of it. Tainted blood—and it gave me away! With everything I tried to do, it gave me away. Tainted blood!"

It came with a breaking hysterical rush, his frenzy persisting even when they had led him aside. The Doctor was still clinging to the table. He steadied himself, stood erect.

"In his blood, gentlemen—though not exactly as I pictured it to you a moment ago. His fellow players told me this morning that this Arthur Jones was of American father—and his mother a native woman of the South Sea Island of Kanaka. He was born in the Solomon Group—lived most of his boyhood in Samoa, It was only a rumor, but my wire to the faculty at Pollin brought confirmation in detail.

"A case of atavism, gentlemen. A sudden reversion—the coming out of a queer ancestral trait latent in his blood. I suspected it—and when I examined Mack's body—examined the wound—calculated the blow—it was evident. The man's mother—a native woman—a Kanaka. The woman's father, grandfather—pearl divers of the Solomon Islands. They carry knives with them into the water; they are frequently attacked by sharks.

"If you have traveled or read of the South Seas, you'll understand. The pearl diver strikes at a shark—a ripping, slashing, upward blow. Not a stab—a queer slash at the shark as it turns belly and side upward to the attack. Always the same blow; they have used it for generations.

"An instinct with this half-caste, Arthur Jones. He was

not aware of it. But, knife in hand, swimming under the water to attack a swimming adversary—in the heat and turbulence of his passion, the instinct came out. He struck the pearl diver's blow—unmistakable! A case of atavism inevitable at such a time and in such circumstances. But I knew that of itself it wasn't enough legal proof—it would never convict, so I had to make this play for a confession.

"That's how it was, gentlemen." The Doctor saw his son coming toward him. "Roy, you—I'm so glad, Roy—so glad I was able to work it out."

The youth's arm went around him. "Sit down, father dear—you're trembling. Dad, I haven't thanked you. I do. You're—"

"I'm quite all right, Roy." With the let-down of tension, the Doctor's nervous energy had evaporated. He sat down weakly. His eyes were moist, but he lifted them unashamed to his friends.

"It's just—a little different, isn't it, gentlemen, with your own son involved? Not so easy to be the calm, theoretical man of science. Roy, phone your mother at once. Tell her I've—I've been able to exonerate you. Tell her, Roy. It will—relieve her so very greatly."

THE MAN IN THE BATH

"HE LAY DROWNED in his own bathtub," said the Doctor.

"An accidental death," the Chemist exclaimed.

"No, Rogers, it wasn't that. I said it looked at first like an accidental death. As though he had become ill—fainted, perhaps—and fallen with his face under the water. Death was, in fact, caused by drowning—the autopsy shows that. Yet it wasn't accidental—it was undoubtedly murder."

There was quite a group of professional men in the private clubroom. A number of club members, most of them friends of long standing; Detective Marberry, of New York City; Detective Magin, of the little Westchester village, Maple Lake; Assistant District Attorney Fraser, of White Plains; and Miss Edith Quealey, a frail-looking, fifty-year-old spinster, of aristocratic face and manner, sister of the murdered man.

The Doctor gazed about the room, his glance ending on the woman. "Miss Quealey, I should like to speak frankly to these gentlemen. If the details will perturb you—"

She was dressed in deep mourning, her face pale and careworn; but she was quite calm. She smiled faintly.

"No, Dr. Adams. I've determined to let nothing perturb me—I want to be here, if you don't mind."

He nodded. "Very well.... Briefly, the facts are these, gentlemen. Less than a week ago—the funeral was only yesterday—Mr. Horace R. Quealey was found drowned in his bath. He was alone in the house—his summer bungalow camp on Maple Lake, Westchester. As some of you know, Mr. Quealey was a retired millionaire. His luxurious city home is in the east Eighties, off Park Avenue. His bungalow on Maple Lake is exceedingly unpretentious—a four-room affair with a single bathroom. He keeps no servants there. Seldom did any of his family occupy it with him. He would retire to it alone—when the city and the family got on his nerves—cooking his own meals, until—after a day or a week, as the fancy struck him—he would unceremoniously return to his home in the city."

"Is all this necessary?" demanded the Banker impatiently. "How did he happen to drown in his bathtub?"

"Quite necessary," rejoined the Doctor quietly. "I'll get to those other things in a moment, George.

"Mr. Quealey, gentlemen, was a man of seventy-two. A small, frail man—emaciated almost. He weighed at the time of his death just a hundred and ten pounds. His health was poor—chronically poor—yet there was nothing seriously the matter with him. He was, to use a familiar term, a confirmed hypochondriac—always worrying and theorizing about his physical condition. The sort of man who carries a clinical thermometer around with him, and takes his temperature every night before he goes to bed to see if by any chance he has any fever.

"This, in fact, I understand Mr. Quealey did. He was also addicted to taking a fairly strong sleeping-powder nearly every night, to guard against any possible insomnia. Dr. Allen here, his personal physician, tried to break it up, but could not. Also, his temper was short. He quarreled upon

"You lie! I didn't do it! I did take a bath!"

occasion with every member of his family; and when these quarrels became too violent, he would retire alone to his camp, staying there until his anger had passed."

"He never quarreled with me," Miss Quealey put in mildly. "Your statements are not quite correct, Dr. Adams. My brother did not get along with his family—no one could. They got on his nerves, as they would get on anyone's nerves. His bungalow on Maple Lake was a haven—the only place he could go to and have peace."

"Doubtless you're right," smiled the Doctor. "I must explain, gentlemen, that this is Mr. Quealey's only living blood relative. Six years ago he married a comparatively young widow—a Mrs. Vivian Mullin. A very beautiful woman—"

"Capricious and domineering," put in the sister.

"Quite so. A widow—she is now forty-five years old. She has, by her first husband, three children; George Mullin, now twenty-six; Robert Mullin, twenty-five; and a daughter, Gladys Mullin, twenty-two."

"And the girl is just like her mother," Miss Quealey interjected.

"Doubtless. This, gentlemen, is Mr. Quealey's family, who, with him, occupied the Park Avenue home. Miss Quealey here does not live with them. On a comparatively small income from her brother, she has her own apartment in Harlem. You will meet these people presently. I have asked them to come here; and then I hope we shall be able to pick the one who is guilty—for certainly some member of Mr. Quealey's household murdered him."

"You didn't mention Mr. Travers," Miss Quealey suggested.

"Mr. Quealey's secretary, gentlemen. Allen Travers, a young man of twenty-eight or nine. He lives with the family."

"How did this man happen to drown in his bathtub?" the Banker demanded again. "Have you any objection to telling us?"

"No, George, of course not. The bungalow at Maple Lake has no house very close to it. But several are within sight. These neighbors all knew Mr. Quealey for an eccentric old man—ill and peculiar. But they all liked him. Last Sunday morning—at seven-thirty, to be exact—one of them noticed lights burning in Mr. Quealey's bedroom and bathroom. The bungalow had been unoccupied the evening before. This neighbor assumed Mr. Quealey had arrived during the night—but lights burning in the daytime seemed unusual. At eight o'clock the neighbor called the bungalow telephone. She thought possibly he might be ill, and, being alone (he usually was, you see), she feared he might need help. The Quealey telephone did not answer. Then the woman's husband went over and pounded on the door. Alarmed, he and another neighbor forced the door. They found the old man lying in his bath, with his face under the water. Dead, and the autopsy showed that death was caused by drowning."

"Certainly it must have seemed accidental," the Inventor commented. "What made them have an autopsy?"

"I'll come to that in a moment. Miss Quealey here is a patient of mine. Through her the case came to my attention. Detective Magin of Maple Lake was first put in charge." The Doctor nodded toward the country detective. "It was Magin who first noticed peculiarities. He mentioned them to me, and I suggested Detective Marberry, of New York. Marberry, who has a bent for the technicalities of science, saw at once that it was murder. Saw also that the thing might be solved by one wholly familiar with physics. Thus we enlisted the interest of Professor Francine." The Doctor indicated a small, gray-haired man who sat nearby. "A member of the Scientific Crime Club, whom most of you know, and, until he retired recently, he was Professor of Mathematics and Physics at Franklin University.

"The case, gentlemen, is one purely of physics, and Professor Francine, we think, has worked out the mathematics of it. You asked me why they performed an autopsy, Mr. Elson? Several small but important details made it look like murder. I shall mention them presently. First, to avoid confusion, I must give you the outward circumstances, so to speak. The doors of the bungalow were locked. The interior was in order. Mr. Quealey's clothes were lying in his bedroom. The bed had not been occupied, nor had the one in the spare bedroom—there are two bedrooms. There was no evidence of anyone else having been in the house. It seemed as though Mr. Quealey had undressed, gone to the bathroom, taken his bath, fainted, perhaps, and drowned. His bathrobe was lying on the bathroom floor.

"Three other details. In the bedroom was his bromide sleeping-powder. He had taken a dose, as was his custom. Before his bath, evidently. The autopsy showed it to be rather a large dose—but not large enough to cause death, or even serious harm."

"But enough to put him prematurely to sleep in the bath," the Banker exclaimed. "That would explain it all."

"Exactly. That is the way it looked at first. Evidently he was in his usual fussy mood. In the water, hanging to the side of the tub, was a bath thermometer, so that he could be sure of the exact temperature of the water. And in the bottom of the tub was his clinical thermometer. Evidently he had been taking his temperature to see if the bath gave him any fever—or heaven knows what idea. At any rate, when he was overcome, or dropped asleep in the water possibly, the clinical thermometer evidently fell from his mouth. It sank to the bottom of the tub; Detective Magin found it intact.

"Those are the outward facts, gentlemen. I have told you what *evidently* occurred. As a matter of fact, we hope to prove by Professor Francine's mathematics that the real events were quite different. Now, there are no trains into Maple Lake late at night; and the neighbors had seen the bungalow dark the evening before. Mr. Quealey thus probably arrived by automobile. But he does not drive. Questioning his family, we learn that he did go out to Maple

Lake in his sedan. The widow and her three grown children tell an identical story. It is this—

"George Mullin, the elder stepson, had been playing golf at his club that Saturday afternoon. He arrived late for dinner, to find all the family violently at odds with Mr. Quealey. The cause of the altercation is immaterial. Relations at dinner were strained; Mr. Quealey was barely on speaking terms with them all. Except George Mullin, who was absent when the quarrel started.

"After dinner, the old man announced that he was going to Maple Lake for peace and quiet. Allen Travers, the secretary, was out for dinner. He played bridge during the evening with friends. He arrived home just at midnight. Mr. Quealey ordered the sedan: ordered Travers to drive him to Maple Lake. The family went to bed. Travers departed with Quealey; returned about dawn—it's a two-hour drive each way to Maple Lake. When the family awakened the next morning, Travers was in bed. They were all having breakfast when the telephone message came from Maple Lake that Mr. Quealey was dead.

"There is the story, gentlemen, exactly as the widow and her three children give it. The servants were in bed—knew nothing of Mr. Quealey's departure. And the chauffeur was ill and away."

"What does the secretary say about it?" demanded the Banker. "He can talk, can't he?"

"Assuredly. And his story is quite different. He dined out, he says, and played bridge with friends until eleven-thirty. This is confirmed by the friends. Then he went home, arriving about midnight. The family had all retired. He says he knew nothing of the quarrel, or of Mr. Quealey's departure. He went to bed without seeing or speaking to anyone. Next morning he learned that Mr. Quealey had gone. No one mentioned which one of the family had driven him, or whether he had gone by an early evening train. Then, a few moments later, came news of the death. And now, says Allen Travers, the whole family is lying and trying to put it off on him."

"There's a lie somewhere, gentlemen, that's evident. That in itself would make us suspect there was more to the affair than an accidental death. No one is willing to admit having driven Mr. Quealey out there."

"Can all the other members of the family drive a car?" the Chemist asked.

"Yes. Each one of them, upon other occasions, has made the trip with Mr. Quealey. So much for what the family say. I don't exactly blame the guilty one for lying, for whoever made that trip with Mr. Quealey last Saturday night probably murdered him."

"What's this Miss Quealey here got to do with it?" demanded the Banker in his gruff way. The spinster flushed.

"Nothing that we can imagine," said the Doctor. "She lives in Harlem with one maid. She was at home that night—had not seen her brother for two weeks."

"You said whoever made the trip with Quealey probably murdered him," the Astronomer suggested. "How do you know that?—how do you know it's murder at all?"

"By several curiously unnatural details," the Doctor answered slowly. "Whoever drove Mr. Quealey out there entered the house with him and prepared to stay the night. To that extent the murder was probably unpremeditated. The chance for it suddenly arose, and was taken advantage of. We know that there was someone else besides Mr. Quealey in the house that night. The spare bed was slightly rumpled, for instance. Someone had sat upon it. Chairs had been moved in the spare bedroom; a wardrobe door was standing open. The old man would not have done this. He never entered that room; it was always in perfect order— as the local servant he employed at intervals has testified. The room was unoccupied so long this last time that dust had accumulated on the floor. The chairs were moved, as the carpet plainly showed.

"Very small—not very conclusive—details, gentlemen. But wait a moment. The presence of that second person was indicated plainly in several other ways—so plainly that Professor Francine's mathematical calculations would seem to give us the exact person. I have never met these people, but presently we will check the figures against them...."

"I said that Mr. Quealey seemed to have disrobed and taken his bath in his usual way. But that, gentlemen, is only the way things looked at first glance. He was a highly methodical man. He did everything in the same way always. In this bungalow that Sunday morning we found his hat, overcoat, and cane in their proper place. In the bedroom his suitcase was neatly unpacked. His toilet articles and medicines were in their rightful places. On a coathanger was his undercoat and vest; his watch was wound and lying on the bureau.

"A methodical old man preparing for bed. Quite true. We believe that he disrobed thus far and then took his sleeping-powder. An opened book was on the bedroom floor beside the reading-lamp and easy-chair. The positions of these articles would indicate that at this point he had stopped to take his bromide, and sat down to read while it took effect. But he took too much. He fell asleep in the chair; his book dropped to the floor. No evidence of a man taking a bath in that."

The Doctor paused slightly. "Gentlemen, the rest of that bedroom was in strange disorder—strange for a man like Mr. Quealey. His shoes and socks were tumbled to one side; his trousers lay in a heap on the floor; his underclothes scattered. Not wildly—merely in slovenly, thoughtless fashion. Doesn't that instantly suggest—"

An attendant at the door said: "Mrs. Quealey and family would like to see Dr. Adams."

The Doctor leaped to his feet. "I was going to speak of the probable motive, gentlemen. It would apply to any of them—his money, and the fact that no one liked him. Quite immaterial, anyway. You will all remain quiet, please. I have something to say to them. They know, of course, that we suspect murder. If Professor Francine's figures apply with sufficient exactness, we will make an arrest. We'll have proof—or enough proof probably to force a subsequent plea of guilty.... Quiet, gentlemen—here they are."

The door opened and the attendant ushered in five visitors. They were introduced informally, and took chairs which the Doctor had placed for them. Mrs. Vivian Quealey, the widow, was a small, slender, fashionably dressed, black-haired Spanish type; as the Doctor had said, a remarkably beautiful woman, hardly appearing as old as her forty-five years. Beside her sat George Mullin, her elder son. He proved to be a big, moon-faced, overgrown youth inclined to stoutness—a ruddy complexion, cherubic-looking, though at the moment he was solemn and ill at ease. His brother, a year younger, was as different as a brother well could be. As George might possibly have resembled physically his big, good-natured Irish father, so Robert resembled his mother. He was dark-haired, dark-eyed, and pale. Three inches shorter than George at least, and certainly forty pounds lighter—a delicate, studious-looking young man. Like his brother, he was solemn and ill at ease as the Doctor introduced them.

The girl, Gladys Mullin, was a small replica of her mother. She acknowledged the introduction in an affected society manner. At first glance she might have seemed wholly composed. But she was not, to one who might have looked more closely.

The fifth member of the party was not, as the Doctor had anticipated, the secretary, Allen Travers. He was Mrs. Quealey's lawyer. She introduced him without explanation of his presence—an alert-eyed individual who seemed to make no effort to conceal his animosity.

"Oh," said the Doctor. "Well, perhaps it's just as well you're here. But where is Mr. Travers?"

Mrs. Quealey answered: "Really, Dr. Adams, we can't say. I discharged the man."

Her daughter said: "He lied about going up to Maple Lake. Mother wouldn't have him in the house after that! How do we know where he is? He's—" The Quealey lawyer abruptly silenced her.

"Well, we'll wait for him," the Doctor commented. "He was called by Mr. Fraser to White Plains, and told Mr. Fraser he would be here—"

The assistant district attorney nodded just as the door

opened and the secretary arrived. Allen Travers was a man just under thirty. An ideal secretary by his appearance, with a quiet, deferential manner. He was rather a good-looking man, intelligent and businesslike; of slender build, but muscular, though in height he was well below average. He came into the clubroom, and acknowledged the introductions quietly and with composure. The Quealeys flung at him glances of animosity, which he returned in kind. The murdered man's sister had said nothing, but her glance to the Quealeys was also full of antagonism.

When the room had quieted, the Doctor said: "I asked you all to come here on a matter of importance. You are wondering what it is, of course. I'll tell you without wasting words: I think we have solved the death of Mr. Quealey."

They gazed at each other in startled surprise. The secretary sat motionless, staring at his feet. But the others, each of them, murmured something. Mrs. Quealey paled under her rouge. Her son George shifted his big frame on the chair and muttered under his breath to his brother, and the brother said: "Shut up!"

The Quealey lawyer broke the tense silence that followed. "That's interesting, Dr. Adams. Is there a mystery about it? We did not want to accuse this young fellow Travers, and yet—"

"Of course there's a mystery," the Doctor interrupted impatiently. "Mr. Quealey was murdered—not to mince words—murdered obviously by the person who drove him up to Maple Lake."

The Quealey lawyer looked at Travers. "Oh, well, of course, we felt that possibly—"

"I did not intend to start a discussion," added the Doctor

more quietly. "We have made out quite an interesting and conclusive case against whoever it was drove Mr. Quealey to Maple Lake. Conclusive enough, probably, to justify an arrest—"

"Arrest!" Nearly everyone echoed it.

"Yes—quite so. An arrest. But you who are innocent have nothing to fear. We'll make no mistake."

The Doctor had been addressing Mrs. Quealey; he now turned to the room in general.

"Gentlemen, as I told you—and to repeat now for the benefit of these others—this is a case of murder—premeditated to the extent that it was planned a few moments before it was executed. I think we will obtain from any reasonably intelligent jury a conviction of first degree—"

"What *are* you talking about?" exclaimed Mrs. Quealey.

The Doctor raised his hand. "A moment, please. If you'll just hear me out. A question of physics, gentlemen. Professor Francine has the calculations with him. Jack, will you open those curtains?"

The Very Young Man jumped to his feet. Across the room, against its windowless wall, green portières were strung on a wire. The Very Young Man parted them. A space some ten feet long by eight feet in depth was revealed. It looked like a tiny stage setting—or, more exactly, like the window of a store selling bathroom fixtures. A miniature bathroom had been set up. Blue-white linoleum on the floor; a bathtub; white enamel bathroom scales, and a small white chair. Over the linoleum, an absorbent bathmat. Lying on the floor, a bathrobe. The large porcelain tub was some three-quarters filled with discolored water, into which hung a wooden bath thermometer. The whole, lighted by a light from overhead.

The clubroom was noisy for a moment as the spectators shifted in their chairs. The Doctor, watching the Quealey lawyer, heard him whisper under cover of the confusion: "Not a word! Sit quiet no matter what he says or does."

"Not so much noise, gentlemen," commanded the Doctor. "I will not detain you long. I have arranged here what you may consider a replica of the room in which Mr. Quealey was murdered. Not exactly like it, but near enough for our purpose. The bathtub at Maple Lake is this size and shape. Those are Mr. Quealey's bathroom scales, whereon he was wont to weigh himself very frequently. That is his bathrobe, and his wooden bath thermometer was hanging in that position. In the bottom of the tub—you cannot see it from where you sit—is his clinical thermometer, which was found with him in the water.

"A simple case of mathematics, gentlemen. Let us take first the suspect upon whom lies the strongest external evidence. Mr. Allen Travers." The secretary sat up at this mention of his name, and flushed under the glances turned on him. "Mr. Travers says he did not drive Mr. Quealey to Maple Lake. He has nothing but his word to support that statement, and there are four witnesses who swear the contrary. Travers can prove with whom he played bridge up to eleven-thirty. Then he went home, arriving at midnight. This his four adverse witnesses agree upon. They then declare he drove to Maple Lake. Leaving shortly after midnight, he would get there a little after two a.m. Mr. Quealey would drive no faster. The murder then—

if Travers is assumed to have committed it—must have been done *after* two a.m.—probably not before two-thirty.

"But was it? Let us see. It was about nine when Detective Magin here reached the scene. If the murder was committed at 2:30 a.m., Magin, then, got there within six and a half hours of it. At nine a.m. the water in that bathtub, as told by the wooden bath thermometer, stood at a temperature of 81. Magin noticed it. Some queer little hunch—as he says—made him remove the thermometer from the water and take the air temperature of the bathroom. It was 76. The previous night had been warm—about 68 around Maple Lake. The bathroom window was closed; obviously the average room temperature during those hours after the murder was not far from 73.

"We then have a tub of water in a room at 73; and the water at 81. The water was cooling off steadily, of course. It started much hotter for the bath. But how hot? I can tell you exactly. Mr. Quealey's clinical thermometer was lying in the water. An ordinary thermometer—such as that wooden one—fluctuates up and down. A clinical thermometer does not. Heat drives the mercury up, but you have to shake it to get the column back. Thus a clinical thermometer records the highest temperature and stays there. This one, lying in the water, stood at 108—the exact temperature of the water at the moment it fell in.

"Thus the water in the tub cooled from 108 to 81, in some six and a half hours, with the surrounding air standing at an average of 73. Professor Francine says that with that volume of water and that bathtub, such a thing is impossible. As a matter of fact, we tried it, and it takes considerably longer. Another—somewhat grisly—factor makes it a greater impossibility. The body in the water had at the moment of death a temperature of over 98, and, proportionate to the water, a considerable *volume* of heat. I need not go into that. Enough to say that the water would not cool so quickly. Professor Francine assures me that some ten and a half hours are necessary. The murder, then, was committed at about ten-thirty to eleven p.m. that Saturday evening. Obviously, Mr. Travers did not commit it, for he was playing bridge at that time with his friends on Riverside Drive!"

A flurry ran over the room, but the Quealeys, under the commands of their lawyer, sat quiet, and with an effort at self-control. The Doctor went on at once—

"So much for that aspect of the matter, gentlemen. I come now to quite a different phase. It deals with bodies immersed in water. In physics it is called specific gravity. Let me explain it briefly. Water weighs, roughly, 62½ lb. to the cubic foot. I say roughly, because temperature and barometric pressure affect it slightly. Also the condition of the water. That water you see there in the bathtub—like the water that was in Mr. Quealey's bathtub—is dirty. It weighs very close to that figure, however.

"Specific gravity, then, is the relation of other substances by weight to the weight of water—the volumes being equal. Placing water at 1, I have here a list of the specific gravities of many familiar substances. Professor Francine tells me the list has inaccuracies, but it will serve as illustration."

The Doctor opened a cumbersome book lying on the table.

"It gives here hammered iridium at the top of the list. Its specific gravity is 23: that is, volume for volume, it weighs

23 times more than water. Gold, 19¼; lead, 11.35, etc. These substances are heavier than water, and they sink. Now take ash, .84; elm, .67; cork, .24—they float. It is not, however, in this case of Mr. Quealey a question of what will float and what sink.

"To proceed. A body floating on water sinks until it displaces an amount of water equal to its own weight. At that point it rests. For instance, in a tumbler *exactly* full of water, I place a cork. The cork floats on the water, but it has displaced some of the water. This water overflows. Weigh that overflowed water, and you will find it weighs exactly what the cork weighs."

The Doctor consulted his book. "In this curious old list the specific gravity of the *human body alive* is given as .89. That is manifestly inaccurate, for human bodies differ. But not greatly, gentlemen. They all weigh a little less than water. Nine-tenths that of water is close enough for our needs. I don't wish to confuse you. You say people sink in water? Only because they must keep the head out. With the head practically immersed, and air in the lungs—the human body floats.

"To apply the cork illustration to that of a human body in a bathtub. If I had that tub over there completely filled and got into it, immersing myself to the chin, a quantity of water would spill out. And the weight of my body, exclusive of my head, which was not immersed, would be approximately nine-tenths that of the water I displaced.

"Do you follow me? Now, suppose I had that tub three-quarters filled. I get in and the water rises an inch or so. If the water chanced to be dirty—as that water is—it might leave a horizontal mark around the tub. You gentlemen have seen it on bathtubs, no doubt—a mark clearly showing to what height the water rose when you were in it."

The Doctor was speaking faster now, and a note of tenseness had come to his tone. "Take another combination of circumstances. Suppose I do not know my own weight. I get into that tub, immerse myself to the chin, and the water rises. The dirt marks its high-level. I get out and the level recedes to where it is now. Then the water needed *to make up the difference* is weighed and found to weigh 180 lb. My own weight, exclusive of my head, is thus .89 of 180 lb., or 160.2 lb. The average weight of the human head is known. Add that, and you will *have my weight.*

"You get my point, gentlemen? Someone took a bath in that water before Mr. Quealey entered it!"

The statement caused a sensation, but the Doctor's dominant voice rose above it.

"Let me finish, please! The water in Mr. Quealey's bathtub had been at a higher level. The dirt marked it. This second person afterward put Mr. Quealey in (he was unconscious, drugged by his sleeping-powder), immersed his face and drowned him—like a rat! That's the way it was done, gentlemen! But the person doing it left a mathematical sign-post saying: 'This is what I weigh. Calculate it, and then come and get me!' "

There was a brief, tense silence. Then the Doctor added: "Professor Francine's figures make allowances for many things I have not mentioned—the water which entered the lungs of the body, for instance. His figures, within his specified limitation of error, are quite accurate, I assure you.

We have scales here—some of you under suspicion may be willing to let us weigh you.

"Gentlemen, Professor Francine gives a possible error of five pounds. And his figures show that Mr. Quealey was murdered by a person weighing 169 lb!"

Every eye in the room turned to the Quealeys. Mrs. Quealey, small and slight; her daughter, even more slender; Robert Mullin, younger of the two brothers, a man obviously weighing no more than 130 lb. And then the elder brother, George—moon-faced, hulking of figure! George had started to his feet.

"You lie! I didn't do it! I did take a bath—you've got my weight right! But—"

The Quealey lawyer silenced him.

"We're glad of that admission, anyway," said the Doctor caustically. "Silence, everyone! Mrs. Quealey, sit down, please! You needn't confess, George Mullin! We don't ask it. Mr. Fraser would far prefer to leave it to a jury."

The Doctor swung to face the club members. "It is all clear, gentlemen? This George Mullin had been playing golf that afternoon. Incidentally, Detective Marberry learned at the golf club that it was crowded that Saturday. Young Mullin couldn't get to the showers. He got to Maple Lake with Mr. Quealey—doubtless with no idea of murder at the moment. He—George Mullin—took his bath. Doubtless he needed it, and the dirt of the golf course soiled the water. The bath-mat absorbed his wet footprints, or we should have had them also. And he used Mr. Quealey's bathrobe, later leaving it lying there.

"Coming out of the bathroom, he found the old gentleman asleep in his bedroom easy-chair from his powder.

Then came the idea of murder. Hastily he undressed Quealey, without awakening him—and carried him to the tub;
put him in it—held him under until he had drowned. A
clever way, he doubtless thought, to commit a murder that
would never look like murder. As an after-thought, he put
the clinical thermometer in the tub. A little touch to make
it appear as though Mr. Quealey had been ill, and thus
fainted. And left the lights burning as they would have
been after an accidental death. Have I got it fairly straight,
Mr. Mullin?"

During all this time, the Quealey lawyer had been argu-
ing vehemently with George Mullin, with the agitated
members of the family grouped around them. As the
Doctor paused, the Lawyer whirled upon him.

"I want this understood now, Dr. Adams—and you, Mr.
Fraser! Mr. Mullin confesses—now, at his first opportunity.
He makes voluntary confession—you understand?"

The assistant district attorney was instantly on his feet.
"You hear that, gentlemen? George Mullin, is that true?
Did you murder your step-father? You wish to confess?"

The young man gazed at his lawyer and gulped.
"Yes—I—I did it about as Dr. Adams described. "I did
it, but—"

The Doctor laughed sarcastically: "I told you so, Fraser!
Good enough!"

"It suits me," commented the assistant district attorney.
"It saves my office a lot of work." He turned to the little
Professor, who with a sheaf of notes covered with figures
in his hand was beaming upon the room. "We have *you* to
thank, Professor Francine—you and Dr. Adams. A simple

enough affair, I suppose, if you happen to have the scientific knowledge."

MANUFACTURED EVIDENCE

"IT APPEARS AN accidental death," said the Optician hurriedly. "Gentlemen, I'm sorry I haven't had time to explain the case to you. They're on their way upstairs here now."

"Who is?" demanded the Banker.

"Milton and Allen Green—brothers. Her nephews."

"Whose? The dead woman's?"

"Yes. She was Miss Annie Snyder, an old maid. I knew her in a business way. She lives quite near me in Maple Grove. Detective Marberry here is consulting with Sergeant Griffin of Maple Grove. Dr. Adams suggested Marberry, did he not, Sergeant? And we've all been working on it. My plan of manufactured evidence—you see, I need you gentlemen as audience.

"Get them here before you—there is no other way it could be done. Ordinary police methods wouldn't work. There's absolutely no— Here they are, gentlemen."

The door opened; an attendant ushered in the two brothers. The Optician was on his feet to receive them.

"These gentlemen—members of the Scientific Club," he said. "I need not introduce them by name— Gentlemen, this is Mr. Milton Green—this is Allen Green—nephews of the unfortunate Miss Snyder who met her death last week. Won't you be seated? Here, take these chairs. You know Detective Marberry and Sergeant Griffin."

The newcomers acknowledged the introductions a little awkwardly and sat down in the chairs the Optician offered. The younger of the two, Allen Green, was a man about twenty-eight. By his appearance, a well-dressed young business man. His brother Milton seemed perhaps four years older. Also well-dressed, though unlike Allen, his appearance was unprepossessing.

Features as good as those of his brother, but marred by pock marks heavily scarring his face. And he had but one eye. Thick-lensed spectacles, behind which the eye showed pale and bloodshot, the other socket closed, red-rimmed and empty.

The Optician said to the visitors:

"You are curious to know why I suggested so strongly that you come here this evening? I'll come to the point at once. The police—Sergeant Griffin here is not quite satisfied regarding the death of Miss Snyder. An accidental death, as the evidence plainly shows. And yet—well, the police do not seem to believe that it was wholly accidental."

He spoke quietly, in a tone wholly friendly. The brothers listened attentively, curious at first, then with sudden perturbation leaping into their expressions. Allen, the younger, smiled a faint smile with an obvious effort at incredulity; Milton sat stolid, his one eye regarding the Optician steadily.

"Not quite satisfied," the Optician repeated. "To be frank, Sergeant Griffin almost feels that it might have been murder."

"Murder?" Both of them echoed it.

"Exactly." The Optician raised a deprecating hand. "Don't misunderstand me, I did not get you here to accuse you—"

The younger brother laughed. "I should hope not."

"On the contrary, I feel that you can help us. And if we of the Scientific Club can assist in solving the case, assuming it is murder, that will help you also, release you of all possible suspicion. You see?"

He was smiling; and they both responded.

"Of course," acknowledged Allen. "We'll do anything we can."

"Go ahead," said Milton shortly. He turned his eye about the room. "Do these gentlemen know the details?"

"We do not," spoke up the Chemist. "But we'd like to."

The Optician nodded. "You shall, Mr. Rogers. To be specific, Miss Annie Snyder was a woman of sixty-three. Of her immediate family here in the East, there are only these two nephews. A rather rich woman—her nephews are her principal heirs."

He added quickly: "I imply nothing, of course. Don't misunderstand me. Merely a fact—an unavoidable fact that there is a motive for murder which makes these two brothers all the more anxious that it should be cleared up."

Milton said: "My aunt wasn't murdered. Look here, Dr. Walker, it's all very well for you to keep stating that murder was—"

"I said, *if* it were murder," the Optician corrected. "We are going on that theoretical assumption for a moment."

"Go on," said the Banker. "She was found dead, was she?"

"Yes. She lived in Maple Grove, in a small, two-story cottage. Her nephews live in Maple Grove also. Allen

Green here is married. Has one child, a little girl of seven. He lives in a bungalow of his own, a block or so from the cottage of his aunt. Milton is unmarried. He lives in a boarding house about six blocks away. Am I correct in these details?"

The brothers nodded. Detective Marberry had left his seat and quietly edged forward, dropping into another chair quite close to the two brothers, but slightly behind them. Chin in hand, he eyed closely their every expression. Behind him sat Dr. Adams. Occasionally the two would whisper together. The Optician, facing them all, went on talking.

Frequently he would glance at the Doctor and the detective, swift, inquiring glances. To the other club members it was obvious that these three were trying very keenly to judge the guilt or innocence of the brothers, watching for the slightest sign from either.

"You'll correct me if I make any wrong statements," the Optician went on. "The discovery of the death came in this fashion, gentlemen. Miss Snyder lived alone, very simply. At seven o'clock one morning the nearest neighbor, some five hundred feet away, observed smoke coming from Miss Snyder's cottage—from a partially opened window of the second story. The house was on fire. It was discovered in time to be extinguished with only comparatively small damage to the cottage.

"In Miss Snyder's sewing-room on the second floor, she was found dead. Lying on the floor in her nightdress. The fire had evidently started in this room. The cause at first glance seemed obvious. On the floor was an alcohol lamp, its glass fount broken."

"Oh, you admit it now, do you?" demanded the detective.

As the Optician made the statements his glance turned to the brothers. The Doctor and detective leaned slightly forward to watch more closely. The one-eyed man sat stolidly attentive. Allen shifted in his chair. Instantly the Doctor gestured. The Optician saw the signal and answered it.

"What is it, Allen Green?" A swift question. It took Allen by surprise.

"What? I—I didn't say anything."

"Oh—I thought you did. I was talking of the alcohol lamp. Well, gentlemen—"

He turned back to the room in general. The incident was over. The Doctor murmured something to his companion, but neither of the two relinquished their keen observation.

The Optician was saying: "This room was quite littered with newspapers. A peculiarity of Miss Snyder's. Though she was a neat housekeeper, this particular room always was in disorder. She was an omnivorous reader of newspapers, and the room was always littered with them. The spirit lamp suggested that possibly she had been ill this early morning—had come to the room with the lighted lamp, possibly to heat water. Had stumbled—or perhaps fainted—and dropped the lamp. And the burning alcohol had fired the newspapers."

"Was she burned to death?" the Banker demanded.

The Optician shook his head. "The body was somewhat burned. The flames were about it. The cause of death might have been that—or more likely, asphyxiation by the smoke—the room was full of it, so much so that the fire was somewhat smothered for lack of air. Either asphyxiation—or perhaps she struck her head in falling.

"She was lying in such a position that in falling, her head could easily have struck the sharp corner of the table. As a matter of fact, bloodstains were found there."

Again that darting glance at the brothers. The Optician repeated: "Bloodstains were found on the table corner—" He paused, then added: "This is thought to have caused death."

The Doctor whispered to the detective: "That surprised him." The briefest of gestures toward the nearest of the two brothers. "Surprised him—obviously. You saw it, Marberry?"

"Yes. Puzzled—he can't understand—"

"You think it might be he?"

"Yes. The other took it normally. But it's too soon to judge. Wait!"

The Optician was continuing: "Such are the principal obvious circumstances, gentlemen. The cottage had not been broken into. There was no sign of unusual disorder. No sign of robbery or anything of the kind. But the kitchen door was unlocked—its key on the inside. This was some-what unusual—the door being unlocked. Miss Snyder was not the sort to leave her doors unlocked at night. It suggests a marauder possibly—"

"Not to me," remarked the Lawyer. "Marauders have to get in as well as get out. Miss Snyder might have gone down and unlocked that door earlier that morning. That wouldn't have been particularly abnormal."

"No," agreed the Optician. "What do you think, Milton?"

The one-eyed man looked up, surprised at the sudden question. "Think—what?"

"Miss Snyder might have unlocked that kitchen door herself."

"Why—yes, I suppose she might."

"Well, where do you get the idea of murder?" demanded the Banker.

"That's what I want to know," put in Allen Green.

The Optician said slowly: "Well, gentlemen, I've told you how the thing looked by virtue of its obvious circum-stances. There were, however, upon closer examination, some very curious things about that room. For instance—this. Miss Snyder was thrifty.

"She bought wood alcohol for that spirit lamp in two-quart bottles. The local druggist sold her one only two days before her death. He remembers it very well. And in her medicine cabinet, that bottle was standing in its accustomed place—but it was empty. Would she burn two quarts in two days? Hardly, when other similar bottles had lasted her a month or more."

"I shouldn't exactly call that proof of anything," Allen Green declared.

The Optician whirled on him. "Oh, you wouldn't? Why not?"

"Why—what could it mean?"

"*I* asked you that! Wood alcohol unaccountably used just before a fire. What could it mean? You tell us, Milton! You can guess, can't you?"

"I suppose you're implying that the fire was not accidental," retorted the one-eyed man.

"Exactly! Wouldn't you reason so, Allen?"

Allen said: "Possibly. Have it your own way. I certainly had no intention of starting an argument, Dr. Walker."

"You said it wasn't proof of anything. It meant that someone started the fire. You knew that, didn't you?"

"Of course I didn't know it," retorted Allen with sudden spirit.

The Optician swung toward Milton. "*You're* not helping us very much. Haven't you any ideas on this?"

"No," said the one-eyed man. "I don't know anything about it."

Dr. Adams shot a sharp warning glance to the Optician. "Go on, Dr. Walker. You were telling us of the alcohol—"

"Yes. Gentlemen, that fire was incendiary," the Optician said firmly. "Someone scattered that alcohol over the newspapers."

"I say—" began Milton.

"Rather far-fetched, you're going to tell me? True. But not so far-fetched either—as I'll show you in a moment. Manufactured evidence always has flaws, gentlemen. The evidence about this room was full of flaws. For instance— those bloodstains on the table corner.

"If you fall to the floor from a standing position and

strike your head against a table, how long do you assume your head would be in contact with the table as you went down? A second? Half a second? Certainly no more. Does blood well out, or even spurt out, from a head wound in such a time? How could it have saturated the hair and stained the table corner in that fraction of a second? An impossibility, gentlemen. Yet the bloodstain was there."

"You mean it was planted?" demanded the Very Young Man excitedly.

"Yes, we think so. A murderer covering up his tracks—trying to manufacture evidence—trying to make his crime look like an accident—might easily be conceived doing just that. It isn't easy for a criminal to manufacture evidence, gentlemen. Something always goes wrong. He gives himself away, for no counterfeit looks like the original when you examine it closely. This murder had a good deal of manufactured evidence about it. And some which was real. The fire was incendiary—"

"You can't prove that," interjected the one-eyed man. "Certainly not by what you've told us so far."

"Well, I think I can. By the alcohol, for one thing. The contents of that bottle had been scattered over the newspapers. They did not all burn. The wood alcohol left a stain as it evaporated. We saw it plainly. Yes, Allen—what is it?"

"I was going to say," Allen began.

"Yes?"

"Well, if you want to argue over this thing—why would anyone scatter alcohol when it would evaporate before the fire started? What good would that do?"

The Doctor half rose to his feet.

"Oh," said the Optician. "Well, that's so. But a murderer

in the haste of the moment, does foolish things. This murderer forgot that the alcohol would have evaporated before the fire started. And he gave himself away! He left stains of alcohol on the newspapers. He thought—naturally—that the house would burn. That's why he started the fire—to destroy all evidence—the body—everything. Then we could never have suspected other than an accidental death. That was his plan. But the fire was discovered too promptly."

"May I ask a question?" the Lawyer put in.

"Certainly, Mr. Rathburn."

"Where were these two brothers when the fire was discovered?"

"Having breakfast."

"Both of them?"

"Yes. Milton was in his boarding house. Allen was at home with his family. Each can prove he was at home. There is no question of alibis—both are perfect."

"Then—" began the Banker.

"Let him go on, George," interrupted the Doctor crisply.

The Optician proceeded. "There was still another very curious thing about that room. Two optical instruments lay on the table, which was near a window. One was a stereoscope. You all know what a stereoscope is, no doubt. You place in it two photographs mounted side by side on a slide—hold its hood to your eyes—focus the slide until the two pictures are blended into one."

The Banker said: "My wife has one of the things—travel pictures—the Pyramids—that idea."

"Yes. Well, gentlemen, that stereoscope being there seemed to us very curious. Either it, or the object beside it—caused the fire! I may mention that a stereoscope cannot be used by a one-eyed person."

There was a stir in the room. The one-eyed brother said calmly: "It wasn't my stereoscope."

"No. Of course it wasn't. But beside it on the table lay a magnifying glass. One of those large round lenses in a metal frame, with a handle. You use that sort of thing, don't you? Either that or the stereoscope caused the fire. By being so placed in the window by the murderer that the rays of the rising sun caught the lens. A burning glass! Focused the rays of the sun upon paper. That's what started the fire!"

The Optician's voice rose to vehemence. "Both these brothers were at breakfast—yet one of them murdered Miss Snyder! The fire started about seven o'clock. But the murder was not committed then. Not at all. She was killed before dawn! The condition of the body showed us that very plainly. He murdered her and set this instrument to catch the rising sun—to start the fire at a time when he had a safe alibi."

Allen demanded angrily: "Are you accusing *me?*"

"I'm not accusing anyone specifically. I want to know whose stereoscope that was, and whose magnifying glass. They didn't belong to Miss Snyder. She was in my shop the day before her death—pricing both articles. She said she had neither."

"It was my magnifying glass," said the one-eyed man abruptly. "I lent it to her—wanted her to buy one. Her eyesight—"

The Optician nodded. "Oh—yes. Well, thank you. That

admission helps us a good deal." He met the Doctor's gaze. The detective said suddenly:

"See here, you two—" He engaged the attention of the brothers. Dr. Adams beckoned to the Optician, who advanced.

"Yes?"

"Go at him strong! It's obvious he's the one."

"Yes. That alcohol idea—absolutely gave himself away. You couldn't miss it."

"Marberry says it's certain. Go after him strong."

The Optician said aloud: "Wait, Marberry! See here, Milton—you say that was your magnifying glass?"

"Yes. Of course it was. And you cannot prove—"

"I don't want to. It wasn't your stereoscope, was it?"

"No. It belonged to—"

"It belonged to Miss Snyder," put in Allen.

"Oh, it did? Well, perhaps so. It was an old, battered affair. You have a fairly new one, haven't you, Allen?" He whirled upon the younger brother. "Haven't you?"

Detective Marberry was on his feet. "Answer him, you damned—"

"Why I—"

"Sit down!" commanded the Optician. "A new stereoscope—don't you remember you bought it off me about a year ago?"

"No. I—of course I did. What—"

"And your old one you discarded. Put it in the attic possibly. Well, this one in Miss Snyder's room was your old one. You planned the thing quickly—safer to use an old, forgotten instrument, than to chance buying a new one."

Detective Marberry had the man by the collar. "Admit it! It was yours—you know it!"

"It wasn't. I didn't have—"

The Optician fairly shouted at him: "You lie! It was yours!"

"Why not admit it?" asked Dr. Adams abruptly. "Dr. Walker is mistaken in his facts. The stereoscope was brought there by Edith—Allen's little daughter. She played with it. Miss Snyder had no use for it. Nor had Allen—because it had no lenses!"

The Optician laughed grimly. "Quite true, Frank. I had forgotten that. You forgot it also, didn't you, Allen—in the confusion of my accusation? Naturally it couldn't have started the fire—since it had no lenses."

Allen had recovered himself. "That's true. I remember it now. My little girl played with it. I guess it was my old one."

"Oh, you admit it now, do you?" demanded the detective. "You admit it—as soon as you remember we couldn't possibly have reason to think it started the fire. Well—how did the *fire* start?"

"Let go of me, you—"

Dr. Adams said: "Started by an electrical device? Or a slight explosion? Or a time fuse— Ah, that got you, didn't it? Walker, you remember we saw the powder train? We clearly saw burns where the powder had been. Get it out of him, Marberry! A powder train, with a time fuse."

"Damn you—let go of me!" Allen was struggling to free himself from the detective's grip. "To hell with your evidence! I didn't scatter alcohol—of course I knew it would evaporate— No, I don't mean that."

He suddenly broke. "You and your damned evidence—I

didn't do any of those things and you know it! There weren't any bloodstains on the table—no alcohol lamp—she didn't fall. I—"

"Struck her on the head with some blunt instrument, didn't you?"

"Yes—that was it. I—I killed her that way. Then I thought I could burn the house—later—after dawn—"

"With a time fuse—and a train of powder, leading to a pile of newspapers. Wasn't that what you said?"

"Yes—that was it. I thought the house would burn—that's how I did it. Your damned evidence—" He turned almost incoherent, but with a flood came his confession.

The Optician faced the room. "Rather a difficult case, gentlemen. Because you see, we knew nothing whatever to start with—nothing but that each of these brothers had a motive for murder. Miss Snyder was found dead—instantly killed by being struck on the head, fracturing the skull.

"It was obviously murder, but there was no clue—absolutely no evidence. She had been dead several hours when examined—had been dead since before dawn—and we reasoned that possibly one of these brothers had started the fire to burn up the house and the body while he was at home with a perfect alibi.

"But how had the fire started? It had burned everything in the neighborhood of its source—we had no evidence that it was incendiary. The body was not on the floor. It was not in that room at all—it was in bed, in the adjoining bedroom. Not a chance of pinning the crime to anyone by ordinary methods.

"Assuming that one of the brothers might be guilty, the case was given to me. Manufactured evidence! *I* have been manufacturing it for the past half hour! Waiting, as I stated these various false facts, for the guilty man to make some sign. It came—quite a while ago. Milton has been acting normally throughout; Allen has not.

"And we knew we had him when I mentioned the alcohol. You will recall that I had said absolutely nothing up to that time about the fire coming some hours *after* the murder. I had not even hinted such a thing. Milton—having no guilty knowledge to confuse him—naturally assumed the fire and the murder came at the same time.

"Yet Allen—thinking I was far astray in my wholly false deductions—confused by my false statements of the main facts—had difficulty remembering just what I had stated. Easy enough to one who had no knowledge whatever, but very difficult for one who knew all the truth. And so Allen forgot himself momentarily. I said that the alcohol had evaporated by the time we examined it—and we had seen a yellow stain.

"Allen then wanted to know why anyone would scatter alcohol at the time of the murder, when the alcohol would evaporate long before the fire. Displayed a knowledge which no innocent man could have!

"We knew we had him then. And when he saw we were accusing him, he grew frightened and refused to admit the stereoscope—until it was proven harmless. Yet Milton admitted the magnifying glass quite readily. Dr. Adams took a leap in the dark at the time-fuse. He was prepared to name all the ways we could think of by which the fire could have been started.

"This whole affair—a test of applied psychology. A guilty knowledge of facts is a dangerous thing to have. A man

trying to hide his guilty knowledge is given to false statements concerning his crime. The true and the false mingle
inevitably in his mind. He confuses one with the other.

"It's difficult, gentlemen, for the criminal to manufacture
evidence. And when you manufacture it against him, it's
equally difficult—for him! He's almost certain to get lost
in the mazes of it."

The Optician smiled at the men before him. "I hope I
never have to try it—for I'm sure I should find it impossible to act normally and discuss false details of a crime I'd
committed—without getting tangled up."

THE MURDER OF MARIA VICENTE

"THE MOTIVE WAS probably jealousy, or revenge," said the Doctor. "These Spanish-Americans—especially when they're young—these love intrigues—the motive is easily imagined—it's unimportant, anyway."

"Three of them, you said?" remarked the Chemist.

"Yes. Any one of the three could have done it—one of them doubtless did."

The Alienist gazed at the gray-haired Banker beside him. "You know what they're talking about, George? I don't."

"I do not," declared the Banker with asperity. "I'm sent for, and because I come a little late I have to fight to get any coherent information whatever."

The Doctor smiled at the group of club members. "I sent for you, gentlemen, because we have a case which could not be handled by the police with a reasonable prospect of success. Marberry here was called into it."

The Doctor indicated the detective beside him. "Spanish-Americans—a young Spanish girl found murdered. When Marberry saw its curious character, he felt that we could handle it best here in the club.... You're right, George" (this to the impatient Banker). "I'll give you a brief outline of all the facts at once. There has been no arrest. I've sent for the three suspects. One of them, we feel sure—possibly two of them—implicated—"

"What *are* the facts?" the Banker demanded.

"Easy, George! The murder took place some three weeks ago, gentlemen. On the evening of Aug. 2, to be exact. In the summer colony of Miramar, Long Island. It is on the south shore, quite a distance down the coast. Miramar is small—a score or two of bungalows and a small hotel. The people are all Spanish- and Italian-Americans—the better-class residents of our Latin colonies here in New York, who go there for a month or two to escape the heat.

"The murdered girl was named Maria Vicente. Twenty years old—a remarkably pretty girl. Unmarried, living alone at the hotel. Had a father here in New York—a fairly well-to-do importer. Maria, it seems, was the sort of girl who gets herself talked about. Not difficult to do in a summer hotel, but in this case Maria doubtless deserved it. She scandalized the old women of the hotel, and, as I say, with good reason. She was involved—fairly openly—with two young men. One, a handsome youth named Juan Melendez, living at the hotel; age twenty-six; unmarried. The other, Felipe Pera, age twenty-five. Felipe is married. He lived there at the hotel with his young wife, Anita—a girl of twenty or thereabouts. A good-looking girl, but nothing like so attractive as her unscrupulous rival.

"Maria Vicente quite evidently was playing both these young men along. Each was jealous of the other, Anita Pera—the young wife—was well aware of her danger. She had had violent quarrels with her husband over his attentions to the other girl." The Doctor shrugged. "A perfectly commonplace intrigue, out of which murder so frequently comes. Maria was found murdered, and, after such turbulent relations with two young men and a jealous wife, we felt we need look no further, either for the motive or the criminal. One of these three—yet we have no way of choosing. And so I have sent for them to come here before you all. They'll be here presently—"

"The girl was found murdered, you say," the Surgeon suggested. "Where? In the hotel? Under what circumstances?"

"The circumstances are peculiar. Practically no clues. But one—the import of which Marberry recognized at once—involves an interesting scientific principle. It is why Marberry brought the case to us. Professor Francine here worked it out for us." The Doctor indicated a frail, gray-haired little man who sat nearby, listening attentively. "Professor Francine has worked out one aspect of the case. And if, by using it carefully before you, gentlemen, in the presence of these three suspects, we can persuade—"

"*Was* the girl found murdered in the hotel?" the Banker insisted.

"No, George. Her body was found on the beach. Floating in the shallow water, as though cast up by the tide. It was found early the next morning. Several stab wounds were in it—evidently the girl had been stabbed to death by two or three repeated blows.

"The conformation of the coast here at Miramar has a bearing upon the case. The houses stand on a fairly level, wooded plateau about a hundred feet above the ocean. The plateau terminates with a cliff—a sheer, perpendicular drop down to the fringe of beach. The houses on the plateau above are scattered. The hotel stands isolated from the rest—in the midst of a wooded area some two or three hundred yards back from the edge of the cliff. A grassy path leads from the hotel to the cliff. Other paths lead diagonally down the cliff-face—the cliff all along here is broken and jagged, the paths precipitous and winding. Some of these give access to the beach—the only way you can get down there.

"The main path from the hotel strikes off to one side and then runs down the cliff. In some places it is so steep that steps have been cut in the rock and iron hand-rails put up. It is all a romantic locality—appealing tremendously to these Latins. This main path, some twenty feet above the beach, runs almost level for a space, on a broad ledge of rock in the cliff-face. It opens, at one place, into a shallow cave, with a projecting bulge of the cliff jutting quite far out above it, overhanging the beach in one place, and the water itself in another—a cave back in the hollowed-out cliff-face, where lovers can sit secure from prying eyes and face the open ocean rolling up on the beach twenty feet below them. A wild sort of spot, that cave with the broad ledge before it; twenty feet down to the sand, and the bulging, rugged cliff overhead, rising eighty feet higher. That Maria Vicente was aware of the romantic possibilities of this retreat seems obvious.

"All we know of the events of that evening of Aug. 2 is this: Felipe Pera and his wife, Anita, maintain that they retired at nine o'clock that evening and remained in their room until breakfast time. Juan Melendez played pool in the hotel until ten-thirty, and then retired. He also declares he did not leave the hotel. Maria was around the public sitting-room until about ten o'clock. Then she left, presumably to go to bed. Several of the older Spanish women of the hotel were much interested in Maria's movements. American women have no monopoly of the desire to shock themselves by prying into possible scandals. Maria had been observed upon other evenings slipping surreptitiously from the hotel, and both Felipe Pera and Juan Melendez had upon occasion been seen to follow her. The older women were always on the watch for such affairs.

"The night of Aug. 2 was black, the sky heavily overcast. No rain fell; but at eleven o'clock a thunderstorm threatened. It swept to one side of Miramar, close enough to give several brilliant flares of lightning. And about eleven o'clock two of the older women, who have a room facing the ocean, saw in a momentary flare of the lightning the distant figures of a man and girl, walking together. They were just starting down the path which leads down the cliff to the cave and to the beach. The flash was too brief to make the figures plainly discernible. The women could not determine which of the two men it was.

"That is all we know of the affair from eye-witnesses. The women watched—but the lightning soon passed. They saw nothing more. Next morning, Maria's murdered body was found washed up on the beach. It was about a hundred yards down the beach from the cave. There were many footprints on the beach above high-tide line—people who had passed along there the day before; there was no chance of identifying any possible footprints of Maria and her companion. No clues on the beach, save one. Further along from where the body was found—almost below the cave, in fact—a dagger lay in the sand. It was just at the high-tide line; no water had reached it during the night. Its handle was buried in the sand, its blade sticking straight up. Unfortunate for us in one respect, fortunate in another. Unfortunate because the moist firm sand had ground off all possible fingerprints from the handle, suggesting that possibly the criminal had thrust it in that way for just that purpose. Such was Sergeant Rance's impression when he saw it. But the blade sticking up untouched by sand or water was fortunate, because there was dried blood upon that blade. Had it been thrust into the sand instead of the handle, the blood probably would have been scoured off. But it was not.

"Unquestionably this was the weapon with which Maria was stabbed to death. An examination of the body showed that no bones were broken—stab wounds causing almost instant death. And the time was placed at something around eleven o'clock or midnight. That is all the evidence we had, gentlemen. The ownership of the dagger cannot be determined. Felipe and Anita Pera and Juan Melendez were immediately questioned. But to no purpose. All three declare their complete innocence. Nothing was gained by questioning them. And then, with Professor Francine's assistance, we were enabled to—"

"Dr. Adams, Sergeant Rance to see you. He has some visitors—three young—"

"Send them up, please."

The attendant closed the door. The Doctor said hastily, "Professor Francine, will you handle this?"

"I think you had better," said the little Professor diffidently. "You see, I—lecturing is one thing, but this handling of criminals—"

"Quite so," smiled the Doctor. Detective-Sergeant

Rance, of Milton Centre, Long Island, entered. With him were the three young suspects in the murder of Maria Vicente. The Doctor greeted them smilingly, introducing them briefly to the club members. Sergeant Rance whispered with Detective Marberry, and sat down near him and the Doctor.

Felipe Pera was a slim, dark-eyed young man, smooth-shaven, with sleek black hair brushed straight back from a high forehead. Well dressed, with a high tight collar, neat bow-tie, a jacket pinched at the waist, trousers pressed to a razor edge, and very pointed, light-tan shoes. A jaunty, graceful youth, immaculate and debonair. His young wife, Anita, was a typical Spanish-American girl. Small and well-formed. A fluffy summer dress, with a light cape over it. Coal-black hair done high on her head, with a small but distinctly Spanish shell comb in it. A nice-looking, but in feature not a particularly pretty, girl.

Juan Melendez was of the same type as Felipe. Rather larger of build, not quite so dapper. Smooth-shaven, exceedingly handsome face. He smiled as he greeted the Doctor—a flashing smile of faultless white teeth. His eyes were dark with lashes black and long as a girl's. Both he and Felipe were smoking brown-paper Porto Rican cigarettes. Behind their smiling, graceful exteriors, both the young men were obviously uneasy. They hung their natty straw hats on a rack and took the chairs the Doctor indicated. The young wife also seemed ill at ease. She acknowledged the introductions shyly, whispered something to her husband, and then sat down beside him. After a moment of inconsequential pleasantries, the Doctor said with sudden solemnness—

"I have sent for you three because the authorities are not at all satisfied with the progress they are making toward a solution of the murder of Maria Vicente." He smiled as though with an effort to convince them of his friendliness. "We feel that you three knew poor Maria better than anyone else did." He raised his hand with a deprecating gesture. "There's no use in my mincing words—no use in our trying to dodge the facts. It was unfortunate for you—all three of you—that Maria should have been murdered out there at Miramar. Your relations with her—no one knows their true details—no one will ever know probably—"

"I have tol' all that I can," Juan interrupted. His voice was soft, with musical Latin intonation; his accent Spanish, with that careful enunciation characteristic of the well-educated foreigner of long residence in America.

The Doctor ignored him. "Probably no one will ever know the real details—the true relation of each of you to the murdered girl. Nor is it important. The principal fact is that, as you know, you are all three under suspicion." Again he raised his hand to check their interruptions. But his friendly smile continued. "Under suspicion, though there is no conclusive evidence against you. If there were, you would have been arrested long ago. Any one of you, we realize, could have had sufficient motive to desire the death of Maria. Love, jealously, revenge—such passions.... Do not interrupt me, please. You two young men—neither of you has seen fit to accuse the other, even by insinuation. You were rivals—"

"No!" exclaimed Felipe. "I am married. My Anita

here—I love her. I would have nothing to do with that Maria. She was a bad girl—"

"Doubtless," agreed the Doctor. His tone was edged with sarcasm. "You were a loyal husband—of course you were not interested in any other girl. Do you expect us to believe that?"

"Yes. It is true."

The Doctor laughed. "So you told the police. And you remember what Sergeant Rance had to say about it? A dozen people in the hotel told Sergeant Rance how you conducted yourself toward Maria—"

Felipe gestured earnestly. "That was all play. We flirt— we Spanish—that means nothing. That is only our way—it is natural. My wife, she understands—" His glance went to Anita. She nodded, regarding him lovingly. Yet she was not actress enough to disguise her true emotions.

"Oh! She understands, does she? Well, she didn't seem to understand at the time."

Felipe said, "I did not even like Maria." He hesitated, then added with sudden decision, "My friend Juan—he loved her. I tol' him she was a bad girl—my wife say so too—"

Anita added: "Yes. That is true. A girl knows when other girl is bad. I tol' Juan she was bad girl—no man would want to marry her—"

Juan nodded. "I loved her. But she flirt too much. That is not good. She had no heart to love anyone. So I give her up. I tell her so—"

"Oh, you did? When did you do that?"

Juan looked vague. "Well, that was a month ago—maybe it was not so long. I tol' her she was not worth my love."

The Doctor eyed them. "You're rather sure of yourselves, aren't you? Well, let me tell you what the real truth is. You're all so involved in this that you're alarmed for your safety. One of you—or possibly two—murdered Maria. Never mind the denials—you listen to me! Let's say one of you killed her. The others either know or guess who it was. You two men were rivals—you hated each other. You, Anita, were angry at your husband, and violently jealous of that other girl. But now murder has been done. You're all frightened—and you've decided that the best course is to stick together, protest bland innocence of any intrigue at all. That's how it is, isn't it?"

Their gazes avoided him and avoided each other. A frightened sullenness had fallen upon them. The Doctor went on vehemently: "If one or two of you are innocent of the actual crime, you're certainly not interested in having the criminal caught. Past hates are forgotten in this present emergency. You're all afraid you'll be incriminated. Isn't that so?"

Not one of them answered him. He laughed. "Well, when I tell you what we of the Scientific Club here have discovered about this crime—"

They regarded him with involuntary, horrified surprise. "Ah, that startled you, didn't it? Well, when I tell you what we know of the real state of affairs, you'll be glad enough to look out for yourselves—admit the real facts—instead of trying to shield each other." He stared at them steadily. "Have you anything to say?"

No answer.

"You—any of you—don't you want to tell me anything more about that evening? You could not involve yourselves any deeper than you are involved already—and you might help me solve this thing."

Still no answer.

"You, Anita—where were you that evening?"

She looked up. "I—you know where we were, my Felipe and I—in our room. We did not ever go out of it that evening."

"So you've said. But *you* went out, didn't you, Felipe?"

"No."

"Well, then, your wife did? Didn't she?"

"No, no! She was there with me—all the time.

The Doctor whirled on Juan. "How about that? Did they leave the hotel, either of them? Don't *you* know anything about it? *You* weren't in the hotel all the evening!"

"I was. I do not know anything. I tol' you—"

"Yes. But you lied! All of you are lying—"

But he could not make them change. They sat now, openly sullen and defiant. The Doctor turned to the club members, who throughout this questioning had sat attentively watching and listening.

"Gentlemen, you see the condition of things? All of them obviously are lying. Half an hour ago I told you some of the details of this crime. I'll tell you the rest now. Listen closely, Anita and Felipe Pera! And you, Juan Melendez! Innocent and guilty, not one of the three of you is telling the truth! Gentlemen, this body of Maria Vicente was found some little distance down the beach from that knife in the sand—and from the cave. You, Juan"—the Doctor swung abruptly round—"you, Juan Melendez, you thrust that knife-handle into the sand so as to scrape off any possible fingerprints! Didn't you?"

"I do not—I do not know what you talk of," Juan stammered. "Fingerprints?"

"Yes. You were clever enough to grind them off in the wet sand—or was it you who did it, Felipe?"

The young husband glanced up from the floor, at which he had been staring. "I do not know anything more than already I tol' you. My wife and I—" He checked himself. And the start that Anita gave was not lost on the watching men.

"Yes? Your wife and you—what?"

"Nothing," he said stolidly.

"You try to trap us!" Anita flared. "He—my Felipe—he is not clever with words. You talk to me!"

The Doctor smiled faintly. "You're more clever, aren't you? Well, one of you tried to get the fingerprints off that knife-handle. And succeeded—the police have already admitted that to you." He turned back to the Scientists.

"Gentlemen, we feel that the murder was not committed down the beach where the body was found. The body was in the water; we believe that it was washed down there from a point further up. The murder, we reason, was committed on the beach near the weapon—ah, that surprised you three, didn't it? You heard Sergeant Rance once say something about the murder having been committed on the ledge at the cave-mouth. He did, but that was merely to confuse you. Both you young men have been seen at different times sitting with Maria on that ledge in front of the cave. Maria liked the romance of that secluded spot. And so you thought we really believed she was murdered there. Not at all. She was murdered on the beach.

"Gentlemen, Maria's body had no broken bones. That

ledge is some twenty feet directly over the firm, hard sand. Had her body been tumbled off there, it would have struck the sand with an impact which inevitably would have broken it."

The Lawyer spoke up. "Might she not have been murdered in the cave, and then carried down to the beach? With intent to shove the body out through the surf, have it carried to sea, and thus disposed of?"

"We do not think so," the Doctor replied. "A difficult thing to carry that body down such a precipitous path. It would have taken considerable strength to do it without bruising the body by dragging it. More strength than either of these two young men possesses."

"Or this young woman," the Lawyer commented significantly.

"Quite so. Indeed, if the murder was committed in the cave, we feel sure that the body must have been thrown down to the sand. And this, as I say, was impossible, since no bones were broken."

During this abstract argument the Doctor was watching keenly the effect of his every statement upon the suspects. All were listening closely, and by their expressions it seemed as though the Doctor's theories were of vital interest. Out of a brief silence, Juan said abruptly: "The murder was on the beach, Dr. Adams? Is that what you are sure of?"

"Yes," snapped the Doctor. "What difference does it make to you? Any?"

"No." He seemed confused. "I was thinking it was in the cave she was murdered."

Detective Marberry, leaning forward in his chair, saw

a swift glance pass between Anita and her husband. The detective whispered to the Astronomer beside him. The Astronomer said aloud: "Dr. Adams, may not you be mistaken about a body falling twenty feet? I'm not at all sure that in twenty feet—even to fall upon hard sand—the velocity of a limp, dead body would be sufficient necessarily to fracture its bones. A freely falling body, under the impulse of gravity—"

The Doctor's smile and his nod seemed significant. To the other Scientists, it was evident that the Astronomer had introduced this scientific aspect at the instigation of Marberry and the Doctor himself. "Ah, there you touch upon a fundamental of the case!" the Doctor exclaimed. "Gentlemen, the question of whether or not Maria's body would have fallen with sufficient velocity to break any bones is vital to us. It also involves a simple but very interesting scientific principle. Professor Francine here has already worked it out. Purely a question of mathematics. Let me explain it to you briefly. Many of you know it already, of course. But for the benefit of these young people I'll explain its simplest basic principles. Are you listening, you three?"

"Yes," murmured Juan.

"I want you to listen," the Doctor added. "You'll find it interesting. And I hope at least one of you will find it unnecessary to lie any further. You who are innocent might just as well admit your movements that evening. You won't be in danger of having the crime fastened upon you unjustly. I promise you that. Have you anything to say now?"

Still they had not. The Doctor added grimly, "You all

three know perfectly well we don't believe you were in the hotel at eleven o'clock that night."

The statement seemed to terrify them all. But they did not speak. The Doctor shrugged. "Very well, I'll proceed. Gentlemen, this problem of the impact of Maria's body after falling twenty feet is an interesting one. It involves that portion of the law of gravitation which deals with what is known as freely falling bodies."

The Doctor gazed smilingly at the Astronomer. "You, Professor Allenton, I know how you feel with me an instinctive resentment toward this man Einstein who would rob us of all the beautiful conceptions we call the laws of gravitation. Celestial mechanics—the marvelously interwoven laws which govern the workings of our universe—from boyhood I have felt the romance of them. Gentlemen, Sir Isaac Newton's laws are good enough for me. And so long as Einstein still remains unproven—I see only yesterday by the papers that those old Michelson and Morley experiments really meant very little—"

The Banker sat up in his chair with a jerk. "Frank, for heaven's sake, do I have to sit here and listen to—"

"You're quite right, George. My enthusiasm runs away with me. This is not the time for an Einstein-Newtonian controversy. As a matter of fact, the practical difference between them in computing this problem of Maria's falling body is absolutely negligible. In a word, then, let me take myself standing on that ledge in front of the cave. The earth is attracted to my body—and my body is attracting the earth. The relative attraction exerted by each of them is directly proportionate to the mass. I say my body is attracting the earth. But very little, of course, since the mass of the earth is so much greater. Now suppose I step off the ledge. The mass of the earth pulls me down to it. I fall. The earth, of course, rises an infinitely small distance to meet me—my attraction pulling it upward. That is interesting, but wholly negligible to the problem.

"When a body is falling absolutely without support, it is said to fall freely. Here on earth—except with laboratory tests in a vacuum—the friction of the air is always a factor; but with bodies of any appreciable weight, it does not alter the result materially, and so we can discard it…. Are you still listening, you three?"

Again they nodded. Felipe said, "I listen; but I do not—"

"Understand what I'm getting at? Well, you will in a moment. A curious thing, gentlemen, about falling bodies. In a vacuum, a feather falls as swiftly as a chunk of lead. Weight has nothing to do with it—except that *in air* the air friction retards the feather more than it does the lead. A falling body, then we find, falls a distance of 16.1 feet in the first second of time. It starts moving slowly, from a position of rest, and is constantly accelerated, so that at the end of the first second it has traveled vertically downward 16.1 feet. I say *vertically downward.* Suppose it is thrown out horizontally? The result is the same. If I throw a baseball *horizontally* out from that cave, it will describe an arc, outward and downward. It will travel a considerable distance in the first second. Two forces will be working on it: the velocity given it horizontally by my throw, which is steadily diminishing; and the velocity given it by gravity, pulling it downward, which is steadily increasing. As one grows less and the other more, the curve changes from almost horizontal to almost vertical. You all know from actual experience just how the ball will act. The point is that these two forces do not conflict or influence each other in the slightest. No matter how far *outward* the ball travels, gravity will pull it *downward* exactly 16.1 feet in the first second.

"Maria's body, then, whether it was dropped straight down or tumbled or flung outward, fell that distance in the first second. It was falling with a constant acceleration, so that at the end of the first second it had attained a velocity of 32.2 feet per second—by which is meant that it was going at that rate of speed at that particular instant. Now let us say, for convenience, that the ledge at the cave-mouth is exactly 16.1 feet above the sand, instead of something like twenty. The body, then, struck the sand with a velocity of 32.2 feet per second.

"At first thought, as you have remarked, Professor Allenton, one can fall twenty feet, even to hard sand, and still not break bones necessarily. But consider the actual mathematics of it. The hundred-yards dash is three hundred feet, is it not? And to run it in ten seconds is fast. Well, Maria's body, with its velocity of 32.2 feet per second at the instant of impact, was moving at the rate of a hundred yards in some nine or ten seconds. Can you imagine one of our fleetest runners, running almost at world-record speed, abruptly dashing himself headlong into a wall and not breaking any bones?"

Silence followed the Doctor's question. He added: "Merely the mathematics of it, gentlemen. This whole question of falling bodies, their velocity, can be calculated to a nicety at any instant of their fall. Mathematical proof—"

"That the murder was committed on the beach," the detective put in.

"Exactly. And, Felipe and Juan"—he whirled on the two young men—"here is something you've never been told yet! You didn't know, did you, that from the hotel one of you was seen with Maria, going down the path that leads to the cave?"

They had never been given this piece of evidence. It frightened them—and Anita—and their fear was plainly stamped upon their faces. The Doctor added: "You three are not what we would call the hardened, professional type of criminal. The habitual offender, even with a low grade of intelligence, has learned to maintain a 'poker face.' You can't surprise him with anything. But you three—why, most of your emotions are plain enough for us to read." It was true. And as he said it, fearful of him now, confused by his sudden twists, they strove for an appearance of dumb stolidity, and failed.

"One of you young men was seen starting down that path," the Doctor repeated: "seen in a flash of lightning. We do not know which of you it was—" He stopped and eyed them keenly, with no effort to disguise his searching gaze. Did his words strike home to Felipe? It seemed so at the moment.

"A man and a girl starting down that path," the Doctor reiterated slowly. "If only we knew which man it was—" As though under a sudden involuntary impulse, Anita opened her lips to speak, but checked herself. The Doctor was on his feet; he took a menacing step toward the girl.

"What—Anita?"

Her eyes fell. "Nothing."

"Oh, yes, it was! You started to say something. That man—you know it was your husband, don't you?"

"No! No!"

"It was! *We* know it was! You and he both—you can't hide your alarm! And look there at Juan! *He* knows it too!"

Juan said suddenly: "It was not I. You said one of us they saw going down that path with Maria; but it was not myself—"

"And so it must have been Felipe," the Doctor finished. "Quite so. It *was* Felipe—we realize that now." He turned on the young husband. "We know it was you—it's written there on your face."

Felipe's frightened, harassed gaze was not on the Doctor, but on his wife. A look of understanding seemed to pass between the two. Anita burst out: "What you say is true! It was Felipe! Long ago I want him to tell he went down the path to the cave that night. He would not. He was afraid they would say he murdered Maria. He did not! He did not even see her that night. It was with me he walked, not with Maria!"

"With you?"

"Yes, yes! He went with me to the cave!"

"Oh. So you claim now that the woman he was seen with was yourself? And you only went to the cave? That's safe enough, because you know now that the murder was committed on the beach."

"No! We don't know about the murder—we did not see a thing—we only went to the cave, my Felipe and I. We were together—I was with him all the time. I want to show him that Maria was bad girl. I thought she would be there at the cave with Juan—"

"Oh. So you admit your husband was in love with Maria?"

"Yes, yes; that is true! I tell you all the truth now. He was—how you say—fascinated. I tol' him she did not love him—"

"And you wanted to show her up? You admit, do you, that you and Felipe went down that path?"

"Yes."

"Do *you* admit it, Felipe?"

"Oh, yes—she tell you the truth now. I was with her—all the time."

"You did not leave her and go to the beach?"

"No."

"But she left you and went to the beach?"

"No, no! We were together—we only went to the cave."

"You did not see Maria—or Juan?"

Both Anita and Felipe looked at Juan. Were they wondering whether it would be best to accuse him? And now the watching scientists saw hatred in the crossed glances of the two young men. Submerged so far, in their common interest to escape suspicion, in this extremity it blazed out.

Juan exclaimed: "They lie! They went to the beach! She—his wife—saw him murder Maria! Down there by the edge of the water she saw him stab her!"

Detective Marberry jumped from his chair at Juan. "How do *you* know? Where were *you?*"

"I was—I tol' you I was in the hotel."

"Yes—and now you're telling us all about the murder. How do you know? Did you see it?"

The Doctor fairly shouted: "Of course he saw it! He was on the cliff—he saw them all down there on the beach!"

The Doctor and the detective were now both standing over Juan. The young man tried to rise, but they shoved him back in his chair. The Doctor exclaimed: "Don't you know it's a crime to suppress evidence? Do you want us to arrest you as an accomplice? You were on the top of the cliff, weren't you? Up there—come on, admit it! What are you afraid of? We know you were up there. There were only two of you men; and if Felipe was down below (he admits he was), you saw him and his wife down there with Maria— saw Felipe stab Maria. Or was it Anita who stabbed her? That's what we want to find out. Don't you know? Why don't you tell us which one of them did it?"

"No—no!" Agonized denials from Anita.

"Yes! I saw it!" Juan burst out. "I tell you now the truth! I follow them—Maria and Felipe. They went down the path—like you said. I did not see Anita. I went to the top of the cliff. Then, in the lightning, I see the three of them on the beach. Felipe stab Maria. And then—"

"That's enough!" The Doctor's sardonic laugh rang out. "Gentlemen, you all hear these admissions! You are all witnesses, and we have most of the truth now! Felipe and his wife went down the path. It does not matter whether they went to the cave or the beach. And Juan was on the top of the cliff. Well, gentlemen—the case hung upon those admissions. The question of broken bones in a falling body was beside the point. I had to use it, because it was necessary to convince these three—especially Juan, as it has turned out—that the murder was committed on the beach. The guilty one felt comparatively safe when that was demonstrated—and we got these admissions.

"The murder was *not* committed on the beach. How do we know? Yes, it was indeed a question of falling bodies. But not the body of Maria. That dagger in the sand gentlemen. Its hilt was far heavier than its blade. Toss it into the air, and it inevitably comes down hilt first—the broad, thin blade acting like the winged tip of an arrow. And in that firm sand—I've given you already the mathematics of it—we had no difficulty in proving—by theoretical mathematics and by actual test—that the dagger fell from the cliff-top. No chance to mistake it! The cave is only twenty feet up—the cliff-top is a hundred. The murder was committed on top of the cliff. And you, Juan Melendez—"

The detective was gripping Juan. "Admit it, you damned murderer! You stabbed her!"

"No! I—"

"You were on the cliff!"

"No! That was a lie! I was not—"

"Killed her and threw her body into the sea! The cliff overhangs the water there in one place; the body fell into the water—that's why no bones were broken—and the body washed ashore down the beach."

"No, no! I tol' you—"

The Doctor jerked the terrified youth around.

"*Why* did you kill her? She had you trapped into marrying her? Is that it?"

"Yes, she—no, she loved Felipe—"

"And you were jealous? What difference? You killed her, and after you'd plunged the knife into her, several times, you tumbled the body into the water. Then, afterward, you found the knife in the grass where you'd dropped it. You were frightened—confused. You thought you were throwing the knife over into the ocean. But you didn't. You tossed it sideways—and it fell down to the sand. Gave us the proof we wanted—"

They pounded him until at last he confessed. When the room was restored to order, the Doctor said: "This was a case, gentlemen, when Sergeant Rance and Marberry had no great difficulty in theorizing upon the correct solution—but in proving it lay the great obstacle. The testimony of those two old women gave us merely a man and a girl going down that path. But which man and which girl? The old women assumed it was Maria. Because of her reputation and because, in that flash of lightning, they distinctly saw that the girl was wearing a white mantilla. Maria often wore a white mantilla—a filmy, creamy white scarf draped gracefully over her black hair, and falling over her shoulders. But we found, Anita has a white mantilla also. It might have been she. More than that, no mantilla was found with, or near, the body. Not conclusive proof of anything, but it indicated the strong possibility that the girl seen could have been Anita.

"Anita's reputation is spotless. If it were Anita going down to the cave, we assumed then that the man was her husband. All mere theories. But then we found that the murder took place on top of the cliff. By Professor Francine's calculations—and by actual trial with the dagger—we found that to be a certainty. Anyone standing on the sand, holding that knife by the blade, could not possibly, we found, plunge its blunt handle to that depth in the firm sand. It could only have got in there, in that position, by falling a hundred feet. More than that; the blade was not standing quite vertically upward. The handle went in at an angle, because the dagger was thrown out sideways from the side of the cliff. Professor Francine had no great difficulty in calculating the trajectory of its outward and downward path.

"Still, by ordinary methods we could not have convicted anyone. It's obvious now that Anita knew of at least the possibility of a meeting in the cave between Maria and Juan. She took her husband there to disillusion him. They doubtless went some little time before the murder—at all events, they saw nothing.

"But Maria and Juan went to, or met at, the cliff-top. Maria did not wear her white mantilla. Naturally enough. She was experienced at clandestine meetings—she knew the white scarf might attract attention.

"For the rest—it was a case, gentlemen, of obtaining from the criminal an apparently harmless admission—which, though *apparently harmless,* was in reality vitally incriminating. How we did it—well, you are all witnesses to that."